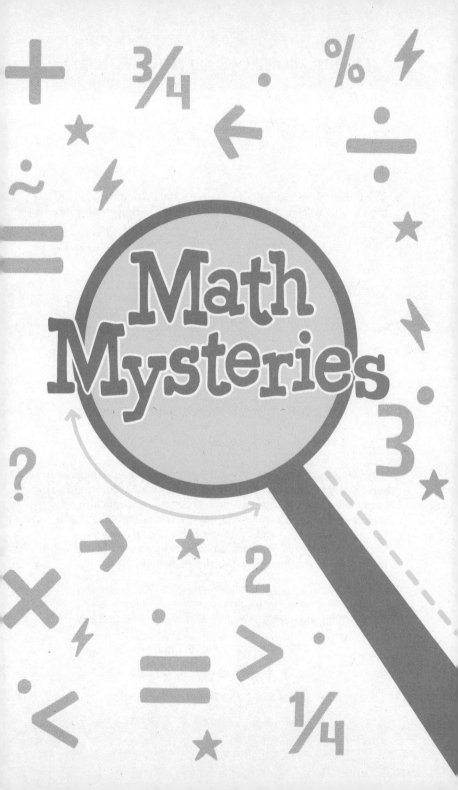

For Mom, who could win any pie-baking contest

An imprint of Macmillan Children's Publishing Group, LLC
120 Broadway, New York, NY 10271 • OddDot.com • mackids.com
Odd Dot ® is a registered trademark of
Macmillan Publishing Group, LLC

WRITER Aaron Starmer
ILLUSTRATOR Marta Kissi
DESIGNER Caitlyn Hunter
EDITOR Justin Krasner
PRODUCTION EDITOR Mia Moran
PRODUCTION MANAGER Jocelyn O'Dowd

Library of Congress Control Number: 2024013061

Our books are available at special discounts when purchased in
bulk for premiums and sales promotions as well as for fund-raising
or educational use. Special editions or book excerpts also can be
created to specification. For details, contact the Macmillan
Corporate and Premium Sales Department at
(800) 221-7945 ext. 5442, or send an email to
MacmillanSpecialMarkets@macmillan.com.

First edition, 2024
Printed in the United States of America by
Lakeside Book Company, Crawfordsville, Indiana

ISBN 978-1-250-84179-7 (paperback)

1 3 5 7 9 10 8 6 4 2

ISBN 978-1-250-90687-8 (hardcover)

1 3 5 7 9 10 8 6 4 2

Joyful Books for Curious Minds

Math Mysteries

THE FALL FESTIVAL FIASCO

ABBY · CAM · GABE

the PRIME DETECTIVES

By Aaron Starmer

Illustrations by Marta Kissi

Odd Dot New York

Chapter 1

THE CASE OF THE EVIL CALENDAR

The leaves had turned orange and red, and the air was the exact right combination of chilly and crisp, like an apple straight from the fridge. As far as Cameron "Cam" McGill was concerned, the new season had arrived.

"Smells exactly like fall," he said, breathing deeply through his nose as he stepped out of Arithmos Elementary and onto the playground. "I'm so glad it's finally here."

As far as Gabriel "Gabe" Kim was concerned, fall had been here for a while. In the northern hemisphere, September 22 was the autumnal equinox, the day when the sun was up for exactly twelve hours and down for exactly twelve hours and when fall officially started. It was now a week into October and Gabe needed to point that out.

"Fall is determined by the movement of the sun and the Earth, not by something you smell," he said. "Fall started over two weeks ago."

"I can smell pumpkin spice," Cam said. "I didn't smell it yesterday or two weeks ago. In fact, I don't think I've ever smelled pumpkin spice in the summer."

"That doesn't prove anything," Gabe said with a sigh.

"Also, it's the fall festival this weekend," Cam said. "There was no fall festival last weekend. So how could it be fall?"

"You're hopeless," Gabe replied.

"No, I'm hope*ful*," Cam told him. "Hopeful that I'll win both the pie-eating and pie-baking competitions at the festival this year!"

Cam's hope wasn't unreasonable. After all, he was a boy with a great appetite and even greater culinary talents. Cam may have been only nine years old, but he was already an excellent chef, and he was learning to be an excellent baker. Only one hurdle stood in his way. Math.

"I can't help you eat any pies," Gabe said. "But I will help you make some. Your measurements and conversions could use a . . . guy like me."

This was true. For Cam, cooking came naturally, and his instincts and techniques allowed him to sauté wonderful fluffy omelets and grill perfect medium-rare steaks. He could look in a random pantry and devise a scrumptious meal in seconds. But baking was different from cooking. It was about more than craft and artistry. It required precision and calculation, which were not Cam's strong suits. That's where Gabe came in.

Gabe had two passions in life. The first was sports. Gabe loved to play soccer, basketball, and baseball. But he was also a bit smaller, slower, and clumsier than his peers, so he was rarely the star of his teams. Gabe's second passion was numbers. He loved figuring out difficult equations, creating graphs, and making predictions using math.

Luckily, he could combine the two passions into a singular pursuit: sports statistics. When he wasn't calculating shooting percentages or batting averages for the high school's varsity teams, he was in the gym or on the playground analyzing the athletic abilities of his fellow fourth graders.

Those skills could also be applied to other situations, including assisting friends such as Cam with their baking.

"I need all the help I can get," Cam said, "because I have to bake at least twenty pies for the contest. There are no official judges this year. Anyone who attends the fair can vote. That's a lot of mouths to feed."

"And I'll make sure you feed them all and win big, buddy," Gabe said, patting him on the shoulder.

"Who's winning what now?" a voice said.

It was Abby "the Abacus" Feldstein. She had stepped onto the playground and joined the two boys. And they were thrilled that she had.

"You're out!" Cam shouted.

"I am!" Abby shouted back.

"How was it?" Gabe asked.

"Weird," Abby said. "But fun."

The weird-but-fun thing she was referring to was a test, and Abby had spent the first half of the day taking it. She had known about the test for less than twenty-four hours, but when she had arrived at school in the morning, Principal Barnes led her straight to an empty classroom and gave her a pencil and a thick booklet. "Leave it on the desk when you're finished," he said as he closed the door.

No other kids took the test. It was given exclusively to Abby. Why? She wasn't quite sure. But it must've had something to do with the fact that Abby could perform large and complicated calculations in her head. After all, her nickname, *the Abacus*, was a reference to an ancient device used for mathematics.

"I'd be a bundle of nerves taking a test like that," Cam said. "Did you ever find out where it came from?"

Abby shrugged. "All I know is that Principal Barnes asked me to take it."

"I'd be way more suspicious if I were you," Gabe said. "I bet it's the government. Maybe the CIA. They probably want you to crack some secret codes."

"There weren't any codes on the test," Abby said.

"What was on the test?" Cam asked.

"Mostly pictures and word games," Abby said.

"What do you mean by 'word games'?" Cam asked.

"Like one question was 'How many nothings are there in a whole lot of nothing?'" Abby said.

The boys stared back blankly.

"I was gonna answer 'none,'" Abby went on. "But then I thought about it a bit and I was gonna answer 'infinite.' But then I thought about it a bit more and I finally said 'one.'"

"Why'd you say that?" Gabe asked.

"Because it was the right answer," Abby said, as if it were the most obvious thing in the world. "You can't have more than one nothing. Nothing is a singular thing. And if you have no nothings, then you end up with everything, right? So the logical answer is 'one.' That was one of the easier questions."

"Jeez," Cam said. "Then I don't want to hear the hard ones."

"We're just happy that you made it out alive," Gabe said. "And that the Prime Detectives are back together again."

The Prime Detectives?

Yep, that's what Gabe, Cam, and Abby called themselves. They were the school's best (and only) group of investigators. And like prime numbers, they were indivisible. That meant they always stuck together. Whenever there was a problem, Cam, Gabe, and Abby would team up and use their wits and their math skills to solve it. As far as heroes go, they were the nerdiest around. And the school—the entire town, in fact—would soon need nerdy heroes like them. They simply didn't know it yet.

It was Friday, and it felt like it. The halls were abuzz with talk of weekend soccer games, dance classes, sleepovers, and of course, the fall festival. Daydreaming was rampant in the classrooms. And out on the playground, recess was especially lively. Fourth graders were playing heated games of four square and ga-ga ball. And Gabe was watching attentively.

Emmett was dominating the four-square court, while Luciana was an ace in the ga-ga pit. This was no surprise because Emmett and Luciana were the best athletes in fourth grade. But their skills were improving even faster than their peers', and Gabe had the evidence of that. He carried a small notebook and the nub of a pencil with him everywhere. And he used them to write down his classmates' sports statistics.

"If you have any extra fall festival tickets for the dunk tank tomorrow, give them to Emmett and Luciana," he told Cam and Abby. "They're sure to make them count."

"Who's in the dunk tank this year?" Cam asked.

"Mrs. E.!" Gabe replied.

"Oh, but I don't want Mrs. E. to get dunked," Abby said. "I like her too much."

"It's for a good cause," Cam said. "Every time someone buys a ticket to dunk her, the charity gets money."

"What's the charity this year?" Abby asked.

"It's called Ricky's Rhinos," Gabe said. "It's run by Maisie's uncle Ricky. It supports the conservation of black rhinoceroses in the African country of Eswatini."

"I've never heard of black rhinos or Eswatini, but that does sound like a good cause," Abby said.

"What's even better is that Mrs. E. said she'll stay in the dunk tank for a whole hour! Emmett and Luciana should be able to dunk her dozens of times in an hour."

"Why not just give the money directly to Ricky and avoid all the dunking?" Abby asked.

Gabe looked at her like she had said she didn't like candy or cookies. "Where's the fun in that?"

Abby shrugged and replied, "As long as she's okay with it, I guess it's fine. My main focus is the pumpkin-growing contest."

In April, Abby had planted five pumpkin seeds in small pots and let them germinate in her family's sunroom. In May, after the last frost of the season, she brought the five pumpkin plants into the backyard and planted them in their own separate garden plots so that they had plenty of room to grow. She covered them in compost, tended to them, watered them, and monitored their progress. In July, she chose the biggest one to focus her efforts on, and for the next three months she watched it turn into a behemoth that she planned to enter in the fall festival's pumpkin-growing contest.

"Do you think you'll win this year?" Cam asked her.

"We'll just have to wait and see, but I will tell you the pumpkin's name," she said, spreading her arms wide. "I call him . . . General Humongulo."

"How big is he?" Gabe asked.

Abby wagged a finger and said, "Not gonna tell. I like to keep everyone in suspense."

"Fair enough," Gabe said. "Speaking of suspense, did you hear about the latest case we've been asked to solve?"

"No," Abby said, her face lighting up. "I hope it's a delightfully difficult one."

"Probably not," Gabe said. "But we need to talk to Sanjeev to be sure."

At the other end of the playground, Sanjeev was sitting on a swing with his head hanging low. He rocked back and forth slowly. He was dressed, for some reason, entirely in orange. Orange baseball cap, orange shirt, orange pants, orange socks, and orange sneakers.

"He looks unhappy," Abby said as they approached.

"He looks like an unhappy clementine," Cam said.

"I'd be an unhappy clementine, too, if I were him," Gabe said.

"Why?" Abby said.

"Ask him," Gabe said.

"What's giving you the blues, Sanjeev?" Cam said. "Or the oranges, in this case."

"Well, everyone is making jokes about me because I'm wearing only orange," Sanjeev said. "That's one problem."

"I'm sorry, buddy," Cam said softly, upset at himself for making Sanjeev feel worse. "I thought you did it on purpose."

"I did do it on purpose, but only because the calendar lied to me!" Sanjeev cried.

"Calendars can do that?" Cam asked.

"What Sanjeev means is that he set a special reminder on his family's calendar, but it popped up a week early," Gabe said.

"Are we talking about a computer error?" Cam asked.

"All I know is that at the beginning of the year, Emmett and I made a pact," Sanjeev said. "On the second Friday of every month, we'd both dress entirely in the same color. So, on the second Friday in September, we both wore all red. And on the second Friday in October, we were both supposed to wear all orange.

The calendar app reminded me that today was the day, so I wore all orange. But look at Emmett."

The Prime Detectives turned their gaze to the four-square court, where Emmett was dressed in what he usually wore to school: a white T-shirt and gray athletic pants.

"He certainly doesn't look citrusy," Cam said.

"Not at all," Abby added.

"Maybe the calendar didn't mess up. Maybe Emmett got the day wrong," Cam said.

"Nope," Abby said. "Today is the first Friday in October. Emmett had no obligation to dress like a tangerine."

"I hate that calendar," Sanjeev grumbled. "Or maybe it's the iPad."

"Before you go bad-mouthing some perfectly good technology, we need to know how you set up the reminders on the calendar," Gabe said.

Sanjeev kicked at the gravel. "Okay," he said with a sigh. "At first, I thought that it should remind me every thirty or thirty-one days. Because I know that some months have thirty days, and some have thirty-one days. But I didn't know which ones."

"There's a poem for that," Abby said, then she cleared her throat and recited it.

Thirty days hath September,
April, June, and November.
All the rest have thirty-one,
Excepting February alone,
And that has twenty-eight days clear
And twenty-nine in each leap year.

Cam clapped in appreciation, but Sanjeev still hung his head.

"I knew about February," Sanjeev said. "But February is still four months away, so I wasn't worrying about that. I focused on the thirty- and thirty-one-day months. I'd never used the calendar app before. My mom and dad usually handle it. But I figured it couldn't be too hard. All I had to do was set the calendar to alert me every thirty days, and once a month I'd be reminded it was time for me and Emmett to dress in a certain color. Because the reminder might come a day early, but it couldn't come late. At least until February."

"But that wasn't really helpful, was it?" Gabe said.

Sanjeev shook his head. "I realized that pretty quickly. Because if I set the reminder thirty days ahead of the second Friday of the month, it would always land on a Sunday, which is definitely not a day early."

"Is that true?" Cam asked.

"Yes, Cam," Gabe said. "Sunday docs not come a day before Friday, or did you miss that lesson in pre-K?"

"That's not what I meant," Cam said, pushing Gabe playfully. "I meant is thirty days from Friday always a Sunday?"

"It is," Abby said. "There are seven days in a week. And there are twenty-eight days in four weeks. So, if he had a reminder every thirty days, it would be four weeks plus two days."

Gabe pulled his small notebook out of his pocket and jotted down a few equations that he showed to Cam.

$$7 \times 4 = 28$$

$$30 - 28 = 2$$

$$\text{Friday} + 2 \text{ days} = \text{Sunday}$$

Cam's face lit up with recognition: *obviously*.

"I figured out the same thing," Sanjeev said.

"So, what did you do instead?" Gabe asked.

"I shifted things back two days," Sanjeev said. "I set the calendar app to remind me every four weeks, or every twenty-eight days. That way it was guaranteed to land on a Friday."

"Huh," Cam said. "That seems like it would work."

"'*Seems like*' is different from reality, though," Gabe said.

"You're telling me," Sanjeev said. "Somehow, I was still a week early. That calendar is downright evil."

"I guess that's . . . possible," Cam said. "Or maybe something just went wrong. But I'm not sure what that would be."

"That would be today's date," Abby said.

"What do you mean?" Sanjeev asked.

"Today is Friday, October seventh," Gabe said.

"Why does that matter if—" Cam stopped himself for a moment and then said, "Oh, I see."

"What do you see?" Sanjeev asked frantically. "What do all of you see that I don't see?"

"Calendars are tricky things," Gabe said. "We've already noticed that with the confusing number of days in each month."

"Not to mention that I never know how to spell *February*," Cam said. "The rumor is that there are two *R*s in it!"

"The rumor is true," Gabe said as he rolled

his eyes. "Not important, though. The important thing is to solve the mystery of Sanjeev's 'evil' calendar. The solution is right in front of us. You're just not seeing it, Sanjeev. It's simple."

Cam turned to Sanjeev and said, "He's right. And if I can figure it out, so can you. You've already told us that most months have thirty or thirty-one days in them. Except February, of course. And Abby reminded us how September has thirty days in it. What we haven't talked about is the number of Fridays in each month. Because, you see, some months have four Fridays in them, and some months have five."

"But there aren't five weeks in a month," Sanjeev said.

"No," Abby said. "But if we look backward a bit, we'll see that the first Friday of September fell on September second. The second Friday of September was September ninth, seven days later. That was when you and Emmett wore red and when you set your reminder for four weeks later."

"I still don't get it," Sanjeev said.

"Go forward four weeks," Cam said. "Gabe, can you draw a calendar to show what's happening?"

"You bet," Gabe said as he sketched out a grid and started filling it with numbers.

"The third Friday of September was September sixteenth, a week later," Abby said. "The fourth Friday of September was September twenty-third, two weeks later. Then the fifth Friday of September was on the thirtieth, three weeks later."

"Ohhhhh," Sanjeev said as he looked at Gabe's sketch.

"So, if we add another week, we end up on today, October seventh, the *first* Friday of October," Abby said. "Which happens to fall exactly four weeks, or twenty-eight days, after the second Friday of September."

"Calendars *are* tricky," Sanjeev said.

"That's why there's probably an option in your family's calendar app to set a reminder for the second Friday of every month," Gabe said. "Sometimes it's easy to do the math, and sometimes it's best to leave the math up to the machines."

"Or to Abby," Cam said. Abby shrugged and smiled. She couldn't argue with that.

"Well, I guess there's one silver lining," Sanjeev said.

"What's that?" Gabe asked.

"I have a week to wash my orange clothes before I have to wear them again," he said.

"Or you can wash your clothes tonight and wear them tomorrow," Cam said.

"Why's that?" Sanjeev asked.

"It's the fall festival, my friend!" Cam cheered. "You could curl into a ball and pretend to be a pumpkin. Maybe you'll even beat General Humongulo!"

Chapter 2

THE TROUBLE WITH LEAP YEARS

The school day at Arithmos Elementary was coming to a close, but it wasn't quite over. There was still math class. Math class was always a fantastic way to end the day and the school week. At least it was for the Prime Detectives. Their fellow classmates weren't quite as excited. They were eyeing the door as Mrs. Everly, who everyone simply called Mrs. E., asked everyone to take their seats.

The good news was that Mrs. E. was a special teacher. That was partly because she rode a hoverboard (or sometimes a unicycle) to school in the morning. It was also because she owned hundreds of unique and colorful dresses and wore a different one every day.

(She was currently wearing one covered in scarecrows.) But it was mostly because she was smart and kind and funny and unpredictable.

"I am invincible!" she cried as soon as all the kids were seated.

The class didn't know what to say to that. So, Mrs. E. said more.

"In all my years as a teacher, not a single student has ever caused me to fall into a tank of water," she cried, sticking a finger in the air. "Not a single one!"

Noah was the first to speak up. "Um . . . o-kay. That's a strange thing to say, Mrs. E."

Mrs. E. flashed a quick smile at him, then she placed a thumb on her chin, stared out the window, and continued speaking. "I can't even begin to fathom a scenario where a student could make me fall into a large tank of water."

Abby waved a hand in the air until she had

gotten her teacher's attention. "I can fathom a scenario, Mrs. E.," she said. "Tomorrow. At the fall festival. You'll be sitting in the dunk tank for an hour."

Mrs. E. scratched at her chin and pretended to be clueless. "I will be? Huh. Well, that's strange, isn't it? But I doubt any of my students would buy a lot of tickets to the fall festival and try to dunk their invincible teacher."

Her ploy was obvious. And it was working. Kids began to whisper to each other, saying things like "I'm gonna buy so many tickets" and "I'm gonna dunk her so many times."

Mrs. E. could obviously hear the whispers, because she smiled a knowing smile and then said, "Well, I guess more than a few of you are excited about the fall festival. I am, too. Because fall is my favorite season."

"Not mine," Sanjeev said. "It's so confusing."

"What do you mean?" Mrs. E. asked.

Sanjeev proceeded to tell everyone about the mistake he made and why he was wearing orange and how he came to hate calendars in general.

Mrs. E. listened carefully and nodded and then did something she often did. She let the conversation guide her lesson, which was another way in which she was a great teacher.

Her lessons were always surprising and inventive. Even the most dedicated daydreamers and door watchers couldn't resist them. Best of all, she tried her best to incorporate the students' ideas and interests.

"Sanjeev's story has inspired me," Mrs. E. told the class. "Today, I want to talk about the sun." Then she walked over to a shelf near the window and picked up a globe.

"*She's got the whole world in her hands*," Luciana sang.

"That's an old song," Mrs. E. said as she held the globe by the base and spun it slowly with her other hand. "I'm surprised you know it."

"My abuela sings it sometimes," Luciana said with a smile.

Mrs. E. smiled back and kept spinning the globe while she walked slowly around the room. "Okay, so let's pretend that I *do* have the whole world in my hands, and let's pretend that Cam, who's sitting in the middle of the room, is the sun."

"Well, I am a shining star," Cam said as he licked his fingers and straightened out his eyebrows like he was about to pose for a picture.

Some kids laughed, but Gabe groaned. He and Cam were good friends, but that didn't mean he had to humor Cam's delusions of grandeur.

Meanwhile, Mrs. E. kept walking around the room, spinning the globe. Stopping back at the front of the room, she asked the class a question. "Does anyone know how long it takes for Earth to revolve around the sun?"

"Sure," Luciana said. "One year. Which is three hundred sixty-five days."

"Yes," Mrs. E. said. "And no."

Luciana's face scrunched up in puzzlement, and that's when Abby stepped in to explain. "Mrs. E. means that we traditionally measure a year as three hundred sixty-five days, but it actually takes 365.242190 days for Earth to orbit the sun. Or three hundred sixty-five days, five hours, forty-eight minutes, and fifty-six seconds."

Mrs. E. pointed a finger at Abby and said, "Bingo."

"It's why we have a leap year every four years," Gabe added. "That's when we add an extra 'leap day' in February, on the twenty-ninth. It's the only way to keep the seasons in line. Otherwise, the seasons would shift slowly, and it'd be snowing in August in a few hundred years."

Mrs. E. pointed at Gabe. "Another bingo."

"But we don't have a leap year *every* four years," Abby said.

"Sure, we do," Gabe said.

"It seems that way, but sometimes we skip leap years," Abby said. "Because otherwise things would shift back in the other direction. So, at the beginning of centuries that aren't divisible by four hundred, we don't have leap days. That means the years 1700, 1800, and 1900 weren't leap years. But the year 2000 was, because it's divisible by four hundred."

Everyone in the class was silent. They stared at Abby the Abacus. Once again, she was filling their heads with too many numbers. It was impossible for them to compute. Sometimes she forgot that not everyone had a brain like hers.

"Wow, Abby," Mrs. E. said. "I didn't even know that! But let's set aside all those extra numbers for a moment and consider something else. What if a year was one day shorter? What if it took Earth exactly three hundred sixty-four days to go around the sun? Not a second more or less. Then what would happen?"

"Somebody would lose a birthday," Cam said.

"Or maybe even three people would lose their

birthdays," Mason said. Mason was an identical triplet, and his two brothers, Jason and Grayson, nodded in agreement.

"Let's assume no one loses a birthday," Mrs. E. said. "Let's assume that the year has always been exactly three hundred sixty-four days. How would that change things?"

"Calendars would be a lot simpler," Abby said.

"How so?" Mrs. E. asked.

"Well, three hundred sixty-four is divisible by one, two, four, seven, thirteen, fourteen, twenty-six, twenty-eight, fifty-two, ninety-one, one hundred eighty-two, and three hundred sixty-four," Abby said.

Mrs. E. had turned to the whiteboard, and she wrote the numbers down so everyone could see them.

EVIDENCE

364 is divisible by

1, 2, 4, 7, 13, 14, 26, 28, 52, 91,

182, and 364

"Remind us again what *divisible* means," Mrs. E. told Abby.

"It means those are the numbers that when multiplied together in different combinations equal three hundred sixty-four. For instance, four multiplied by ninety-one equals three hundred sixty-four. So does thirteen multiplied by twenty-eight."

$$4 \times 91 = 364$$

$$13 \times 28 = 364$$

"And how is that helpful?" Mrs. E. said.

"If the year was three hundred sixty-four days, then you'd have lots of easy options," Abby said. "If you kept a week as seven days, you could have exactly fifty-two weeks in a year. You could have four seasons that each contained thirteen weeks, or ninety-one days a season. Months could be exactly twenty-eight days, or exactly four weeks. And you could have exactly thirteen months per year."

$$7 \underset{\substack{\text{DAYS} \\ \text{PER WEEK}}}{} \times 52 \underset{\text{WEEKS}}{} = 364 \underset{\text{DAYS}}{}$$

$$7 \underset{\substack{\text{DAYS} \\ \text{PER WEEK}}}{} \times 13 \underset{\substack{\text{WEEKS} \\ \text{PER SEASON}}}{} = 91 \underset{\substack{\text{DAYS} \\ \text{PER SEASON}}}{} \rightarrow 91 \underset{\substack{\text{DAYS} \\ \text{PER SEASON}}}{} \times 4 \underset{\text{SEASONS}}{} = 364 \underset{\text{DAYS}}{}$$

$$7 \underset{\substack{\text{DAYS} \\ \text{PER WEEK}}}{} \times 4 \underset{\substack{\text{WEEKS} \\ \text{PER MONTH}}}{} = 28 \underset{\substack{\text{DAYS} \\ \text{PER MONTH}}}{} \rightarrow 28 \underset{\substack{\text{DAYS} \\ \text{PER MONTH}}}{} \times 13 \underset{\text{MONTHS}}{} = 364 \underset{\text{DAYS}}{}$$

$$\rightarrow 364 \text{ days}$$

Mrs. E. wrote it all out as equation.

Gabe caught on quickly, and said, "So, if the first of January fell on a Monday, then the first of every month would fall on a Monday, and—"

"You'd always know which day would be the second Friday of the month because it would always be the same!" Sanjeev butted in to say.

Gabe elaborated even further. "Which means Christmas would always be on the same day of the week. So would every holiday. Each day of the week would always fall on the same numbered day, no matter what month it was. For instance, Mondays would be on the first, eighth, fifteenth, and twenty-second days of every month."

"A month would be closer to the actual moon cycle, too," Luciana said. "It takes just under twenty-eight days for the moon to go around Earth."

"You're all correct," Mrs. E. said as she set the globe down on Maisie's desk. "Cool, right?"

"Confusing is more like it," Maisie said. "Why do we have to change things that were already working perfectly fine?"

Cam shook his head and proclaimed, "I disagree. I think change is good. I say we do it."

"I'm not sure we can change Earth's orbit," Gabe said with a grumble.

"Yeah, and Mason, Jason, and I were born on the thirty-first of March," Grayson said. "Would our birthday disappear?"

"Plus, you said there would be thirteen months," Noah said. "What about this new month? What would we call it?"

"I say we call it Thirtember!" Cam said. "Or Bonusary!"

"What about Awesomesaurus?" Emmett said. "I know it sounds more like a dinosaur, but that's what makes it cool."

"How about we call it Luciana?" Luciana said.

"You can't call a month by a person's name," Jason said.

"There are people named April, May, June, July, and August who'd say you're wrong about that," Luciana said. It was a good point.

"We can figure out a name for the new month when we change the orbit of Earth around the sun and when we convince the entire world to change the calendars," Mrs. E. said. "But this is all to illustrate a point. As humans, we try to make sense of the universe as best we can. We try to fit things into perfect boxes. But sometimes our boxes are a bit too big or a bit too small. Because the universe doesn't care. The universe does what the universe wants."

"Then the universe must be out to get me," Kiko groaned.

Everyone turned around to look at her. She was sitting in the back row of the classroom with her head in her hands. She let out a huge sigh, the type of hopeless exclamation that usually meant one thing. The Prime Detectives would soon have a new case to solve.

Before delving into the reason for Kiko's distress, it's important to understand a few things about Arithmos Elementary and the

Prime Detectives. The Prime Detectives hadn't always been the Prime Detectives. In first and second grade, Abby and Cam were friends, but they didn't have any grand ambitions to solve mysteries. It wasn't until third grade, when Gabe moved into town, that the three became inseparable. They found their skills and personalities were a perfect match for figuring out any issue, big or small, that plagued their school.

Abby was a whiz with numbers, of course, but her laid-back nature also helped her see the big picture more clearly than the two boys, who were sometimes too swept up in the emotions and minor details of a case. Those distractions weren't always a bad thing, though. In fact, most of the time, they were a good thing.

Cam's empathy was a strength that made up for his still-developing math skills. He was goofy, sure, but he was also extremely personable. When a witness talked, he listened. And when a suspect was hesitant to talk, he asked the right questions to uncover their motives. In short, he understood people.

Gabe was far pricklier than Cam and Abby, but he was also more focused on the fine points of a case, on getting the job done. His math skills were better than most, but his determination was unmatched. He never, ever gave up.

Becoming the Prime Detectives was never a plan for the trio. It simply happened one day in third grade. There was nothing particularly notable about the day. The only difference was that their classmate Emmett, who seemed a bit upset, joined them at their lunch table. When Cam asked Emmett why he looked "so glum," Emmett explained that he couldn't find his backpack.

Through perceptive questions about morning routines, Cam quickly figured out that Emmett probably left the backpack in the cafeteria while he was picking up his morning breakfast. After all, the cafeteria was a place where Cam often lost things, too. It was lunchtime, and the backpack was no longer there, so Cam decided that the backpack must be "waiting for you at the lost-and-found."

"Already checked," Emmett said with a sigh. "No luck."

That's when Gabe stepped in. He determined that the backpack could've been accidentally picked up by one of their schoolmates. Gabe asked Emmett what time he got his breakfast and how long the line was. Gabe then used that information to determine how many kids might've gotten breakfast after Emmett and then mistakenly picked up the backpack.

Abby took over from there. In an instant, she narrowed down the suspects by calculating which students would've had a bag of a similar weight and size and which ones would've been at the back of the morning line due to bus schedules and traffic patterns. In moments, she was pointing across the cafeteria at their classmate Noah.

"He has it," she said.

Then they walked over to Noah and asked him to show them his backpack. Everyone, including Noah, immediately recognized the mistake. He had Emmett's backpack! Then they quickly determined that Noah had left his own backpack (which was the same color and style as Emmett's) on the bus.

"Wow," Emmett said. "You solved two mysteries in, like, two minutes. You should start a detective agency and charge people."

At the same time, Abby, Cam, and Gabe all turned to one another with wide eyes. And Abby was the first to speak. "Your smiles are good enough payment for me," she said. "Solving mysteries is fun."

Cam and Gabe had nodded in agreement. From that point on, they were the kids that other kids turned to whenever they had a problem. And they wouldn't accept anything but smiles once the case was closed. Abby, Cam, and Gabe were the best. And they were inseparable. They were, quite simply, the Prime Detectives.

Now, the Prime Detectives had yet another case to solve.

Kiko's case. The one that was making her so upset. Only they didn't know what Kiko's case was yet. She claimed the universe was out to get her. The universe would be a difficult suspect to apprehend. Obviously, they needed more information. So, they waited for her to provide it.

Kiko was a small girl with large glasses and a big heart. She also had a tiny purse with a zipper across the top. Clutching it like it was a prized toy, Kiko continued to sulk.

"Kiko," Mrs. E. said. "What's going on?"

Kiko sniffled, then wiped a tear from her cheek with her arm. She continued to clutch her purse. "All I know is that most of my money is gone," she said. "And now I don't have enough money left over to buy tickets for the fall festival."

Tipping her purse upside down resulted in nothing but a few coins falling onto Kiko's desk and bouncing to the floor. Gabe scrambled to scoop them up and deposited them back on her desk in a small stack.

"One dollar and fifty-one cents," he said. "Six quarters and a penny. Is that all of it?"

Kiko nodded.

"And how much should you have?" Abby asked.

"I left the house with a twenty-dollar bill," Kiko said. "And I should've had six dollars and fifty-one cents left over, which would be enough to buy three tickets to use for lemonade and games at the fall festival. But now I can't even buy a single ticket because they're two dollars apiece."

"So, you're missing five dollars?" Gabe asked. "No wonder you're upset."

"Did you check to see if there's a hole in

the bottom of your purse?" Cam said. "All my pockets have at least one hole in them."

"All pockets have at least one hole in them," Gabe said. "That's what makes them pockets."

"You know what I mean," Cam said.

"The only hole in my purse is the one I can zip up," Kiko said. "But I did spend a lot of money today, so it feels like cash was dropping out of the bottom."

"Interesting," Abby said. "Did anyone else hold your purse at any point?"

Kiko shook her head. "Unless they took it from me when I wasn't looking and then slipped it back into my backpack."

Gabe's eyes scanned the class, checking to see if anyone was hiding their face or acting nervous. Was it possible that there was a thief in their midst? And if there was, would he be able to tell who?

Cam took a more direct approach.

"Hey, everyone!" Cam said to the class. "Did any of you snatch Kiko's purse, pilfer five dollars from it, and then slip it back into her backpack without her noticing?"

No one responded, so Gabe took over again.

"I'm not a lawyer," he said. "But I bet if the guilty party returned the money and said they were sorry, they wouldn't spend too much time in jail."

"Jail!" Mason shouted. "Are you serious?"

Gabe shrugged and said, "You do the crime, you do the time."

"I don't think anyone is going to jail," Mrs. E. said. "I'm sure there's an explanation besides a master thief."

"Do you think it was aliens or time travelers?" Jason asked. "I bet they could steal five dollars."

"Seriously?" Gabe said. "Have you ever heard of Occam's razor?"

"I don't have a beard yet, so no, I haven't heard of that guy's razor," Jason said.

"Occam's razor isn't an actual razor," Abby said. "It's a problem-solving principle. It states that 'entities are not to be multiplied without necessity.'"

"What does that have to do with aliens and time travelers?" Mason asked.

"Nothing," Gabe said. "She means that we shouldn't overcomplicate things. Simple answers are usually the most likely answers."

"So how do we figure out the simple answer?" Kiko said.

"Maybe with math," Cam said.

"Probably with math," Gabe said.

"Definitely with math," Abby said.

Chapter 3

THE CASE OF THE FIVE DOLLARS THAT JUST . . . FLOATED AWAY

Mrs. E. fired the whiteboard back up. She had only known the Prime Detectives for a few weeks, but she knew them well enough to realize that they were about to start spouting off equations. For the sake of the other kids in the class, she would write the equations down and then everyone could follow what was happening.

"So, what sort of math are we doing today?" Mrs. E. asked.

"That depends," Gabe said. "We need more information from Kiko."

"Don't look at me," Kiko said, throwing up her hands. "I don't know what math equations you should use."

"Don't worry about that," Abby said.

"Yeah," Cam added. "Just tell us about your day, and we'll figure out where your five dollars went."

"Okay," Kiko said. "So, what do you want to know?"

"Start with this morning," Gabe said. "When you had all your money."

"Okay," Kiko said.

"As I told you, I left the house with a twenty-dollar bill. On my walk to school, I decided that I wanted a chocolate croissant."

"Always a wise decision," Cam said.

"So, I stopped by Bertha's Bakery, and I bought one for four dollars," Kiko said.

"Was that four dollars plus sales tax?" Abby asked.

"Good point," Gabe said. "When they gave you your change, did it include coins, or just bills?"

Kiko thought about it for a moment and then said, "There were coins, too."

"So, that means you paid tax," Gabe said.

"And as anyone who's ever stepped into a store with a five-dollar bill hoping to buy something fun knows,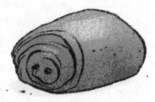

the store will actually charge you more than the five dollars marked on a price tag. Six percent more, to be precise. That's the local sales tax rate. So Bertha's Bakery would have charged you—"

"Four dollars and twenty-four cents," Abby said instantly. "And since you gave them a twenty, they should've given you fifteen dollars and seventy-six cents in change."

"Let's work through how you figured that out so that everyone understands," Mrs. E. said. "How did you calculate the tax?"

"If a tax rate is six percent, then you have to multiply six percent by the price of the item and add that result to the original price," Abby said.

"So, if something costs one dollar, what do you do?" Mrs. E. asked.

"That's an easy one," Gabe said. "Six percent can be written with a decimal point. It's zero point zero six. And one dollar is the same as one hundred cents."

Mrs. E. wrote it on the board.

EVIDENCE

6% = 0.06

$1 = 100
cents

"So, we multiply one hundred cents by zero point zero six, and we get six cents," Gabe said. "We're basically multiplying one hundred by six and then moving the decimal point two spaces to the left."

Mrs. E. kept writing.

$$100 \underset{\text{cents}}{} \times 0.06 = 6 \underset{\text{cents}}{}$$

"We add those six cents to the original dollar, and we get one dollar and six cents."

$$\$1 + \$0.06 = \$1.06 \text{ or } 1 \underset{\text{dollar}}{} \text{ and } 6 \underset{\text{cents}}{}$$

"But I spent four dollars plus tax," Kiko said.

"Right," Mrs. E. said. "So how do we do four dollars?"

"Just do the equation with four instead of one," Gabe said.

"Like this?" Mrs. E. asked. And then she wrote the following on the board.

$$\$4 = 400 \underset{\text{cents}}{}$$
$$400 \times 0.06 = 24 \underset{\text{cents}}{}$$
$$\$4 + \$0.24 = \$4.24$$

"Right," Abby said. "And to figure out the change Kiko should've received, we just subtract that number from her twenty-dollar bill, and we get fifteen dollars and seventy-six cents."

$$\$20.00 - \$4.24 = \$15.76$$

"I didn't count my change, but that sounds right," Kiko said. "They gave me a ten first, then a five, and then some coins."

"What next?" Cam asked.

"Next I ran into Maisie on the front steps of the school," Kiko said. "She bought me a chocolate croissant from Bertha's Bakery yesterday, so I paid her back."

"With the tax added?" Gabe asked.

Kiko hung her head. "I forgot about that. We were both late and in a rush to get inside, so I just gave her five dollars and she gave me one dollar in change. I guess I still owe her twenty-four cents."

"That's for you and her to figure out later," Gabe said. "But we know that fifteen dollars and seventy-six cents minus four dollars equals eleven dollars and seventy-six cents. Easy."

$$\$15.76 - \$4.00 = \$11.76$$

"Clear enough," Cam said. "But you still have plenty of money at this point. So, what happened next?"

"Well, I bought a Laser Dog comic book from Noah for two dollars and twenty-five cents," Kiko said. "That's what happened next."

Mrs. E. didn't even wait for the Prime Detectives to do the calculation. She simply wrote it on the whiteboard.

$$\$11.76 - \$2.25 = \$9.51$$

"That's a good deal for a Laser Dog comic," Cam said, nodding approvingly.

"It really is," Kiko said. "But I used my last five-dollar bill to pay for it. And then, later today, when I bought a box of Adventure Scout Cookies from Isabella for three dollars, I used my last three one-dollar bills. I was left with what I have right now. Which is one dollar and fifty-one cents in change."

"You should have six dollars and fifty-one cents, though," Abby said.

"Abby is right, of course," Mrs. E. said, and she showed the work.

$$\$9.51 - \$3.00 = \$6.51$$

"Exactly," Kiko said. "I knew I should've had enough money left for three tickets to the fall festival, but I was five dollars short. So, what happened?"

Abby shrugged. "Got me stumped. The math is all correct."

"Stumped me, too," Gabe said. "I still think it's possible you got robbed."

"Or . . . ," Cam said, standing up and creating a moment of anticipation. He was a showman at heart.

"Or what?" multiple kids called out.

"Or . . . maybe we all should've listened to what Kiko actually told us," Cam said.

Gabe's face scrunched up in offense. "But we did listen to her."

"You listened to the numbers and did the calculations, but you didn't listen to the words," Cam said.

"How so?" Abby asked.

"Yeah, what was I saying that everyone missed?" Kiko said.

"Okay," Cam said. "Let me break it down. You started the day with a twenty-dollar bill, right?"

"Right," Kiko said.

"You gave that twenty to the bakery, and they gave you change that included a ten-dollar bill, a five, and some coins, correct?"

"Yes," Kiko said. "And the ten-dollar bill had a drawing on it. A little panda!"

"That's very good to know," Cam said. "But let's talk about what happened next. You paid Maisie back four dollars, right? You gave her five dollars and she gave you a dollar in change. Is that correct?"

"Yep," Kiko said. "Then I bought the Laser Dog comic book from Noah for two dollars and twenty-five cents."

"Laser Dog comics are the best," Cam said.

"I think so, too!" Kiko said.

"And you paid for the comic with another five-dollar bill, right?" Cam said.

Kiko nodded. "Noah saw Abraham Lincoln on the bill and made a joke about how Laser Dog should run for president in the next issue."

"The change was two dollars and seventy-five cents, correct?" Cam asked.

"Correct," Kiko said.

"Okay," Cam said. "And then finally you bought Adventure Scout Cookies from Isabella for three dollars, which were your last three one-dollar bills. Leaving you with six quarters and one penny for a total of one dollar and fifty-one cents."

"Exactly," Kiko said.

"So, then it's obvious what happened," Cam said.

"It is?" Gabe, Abby, and Kiko all said at the same time.

"Yeah," Cam said. "But first I need to ask Maisie something."

"Me?" Maisie said, looking up in surprise. Mrs. E. had left the globe on Maisie's desk, and Maisie had been distracted by it, spinning it around and examining the geography up close. Until Cam had mentioned her name, Maisie had seemed oblivious to the mystery that he was solving.

"Do you have your purse or wallet or whatever you carry money in with you?" Cam asked her.

Maisie stumbled through her response. "Um . . . I . . . It's in my backpack. I think? Why does that—?"

Before Maisie could say another word, Kiko stood from her desk, reached into her own wallet, and said, "I still owe you that sales tax." Then she pulled out one of her six quarters. "Even though I only owe you twenty-four cents, I want you to keep the change."

Kiko handed Maisie the quarter and looked down into her wallet and sighed.

Maisie's eyebrows went up as she took the quarter. "Wow. That's really honest of you. And generous. Thank you."

"It's only some change," Kiko said. "It's not going to get me tickets for the fall festival."

"Maybe not," Cam said, and he reached into his pocket and pulled out two five-dollar bills. "But one of these five-dollar bills will be yours soon enough."

"Wait," Kiko said. "You didn't steal my money, did you?"

"No," Cam said. "But I want Maisie to give me a ten-dollar bill for my two five-dollar bills."

"But I don't have a ten-dollar bill," Maisie said.

"Sure you do," Cam said. "You have one with a drawing of a panda on it."

Maisie looked at him sideways, then reached down with her left hand and unzipped her backpack. She pulled out an envelope filled with what looked like a fair amount of cash. It had the word FESTIVAL written on it.

"I don't have any tens," she said. "Only twenties and the five Kiko gave me."

But when she pulled the top bill out of the envelope, she was proved wrong. Because there in her left hand was a ten-dollar bill. And on the ten-dollar bill was a drawing of a panda.

"Wait a second," Kiko said. "That's the ten-dollar bill I got at Bertha's Bakery."

"And it's the ten-dollar bill that you gave Maisie," Cam said. "By mistake."

"How'd you know that?" Gabe asked.

"Because I listened to what Kiko told us," Cam replied. "When Kiko first got her change from Bertha's Bakery, they gave her one ten-dollar bill and one five-dollar bill, plus some coins. She said she paid Maisie with a five-dollar bill and received one dollar in change. Then she said she paid Noah with a five-dollar bill and received two dollars and seventy-five cents in change. Both can't be true. Because she only had one five-dollar bill to start with!"

"Oh my gosh," Gabe said. "How did I not notice that?"

"How'd you know she gave the ten dollars to Maisie and not Noah?" Abby asked.

"Again, listening," Cam said. "I knew she didn't give the ten dollars to Noah because he made a joke about presidents and Abraham Lincoln, who's on the five-dollar bill. Alexander Hamilton, who was never a president, is on the ten. So, it had to be Maisie."

"Oh my," Maisie said to Kiko. "We were in such a rush when you paid me back that I didn't notice. I'm so sorry. How can I repay you?"

"Like this," Cam said, and he handed one of his five-dollar bills to Kiko and one to Maisie. Then he took the ten-dollar panda bear bill from Maisie's hand and slipped it into his pocket.

The class sat in stunned silence for a few moments. Until Gabe nodded at his friend and started clapping, which made Cam smile as wide as he'd ever smiled before.

Beaming, Abby clapped as well, followed by the entire class.

Finally, Mrs. E. clapped louder than everyone, and she said, "Wonderful job, Cam. I'm so glad that's settled. I didn't expect a panda to help save the day, but never underestimate animals. Pandas used to be close to extinction, you know. But thanks to conservation efforts, they're thriving again."

Mrs. E. was an avowed animal lover and had the pets to prove it. Back at the farmhouse she owned with her husband, they had four dogs, six cats, five chickens, two goats, one rabbit, one iguana, eight hamsters, three snakes, two ferrets, and one budgie.

"Speaking of conservation efforts, I was hoping that Maisie could tell us more about her uncle's work with the black rhinoceroses of Eswatini," Abby said.

The class turned to Maisie. She placed her left hand on the globe, covering the continent of Africa. Blushing, she said, "I'm not sure what there is to say."

"I say we go make a difference," Cam said as he stood up and started walking toward the door.

"Where are you going?" Mrs. E. asked.

"To save the black rhinoceroses of Eswatini!" Cam called back, then he pointed up at the clock.

"The last bell will ring in five seconds, and I want to be first in line to buy my tickets to the fall festival."

As soon as he stopped talking, the bell rang. The school day was over.

Chapter 4

PUNKIN' CHUNKIN'

A booth selling tickets to the fall festival sat outside the school next to the buses. Kids who had money on them, like Kiko and Cam, took advantage of the opportunity to buy their tickets at a discount from the booth. There would still be an opportunity to buy tickets the next morning at the festival itself. But instead of two dollars, they would cost three dollars apiece. The price of procrastination.

Cam bought five tickets with his ten-dollar panda bill. Kiko happily purchased her three tickets. And other kids picked up anywhere from one to ten tickets. Maisie, representing her uncle Ricky, was behind the booth with her older sister, Haley. She did her best to drum up the most cash, reminding the students that "if you buy your tickets tomorrow, then more money will go to Ricky's Rhinos."

A few people, including Abby and Gabe, opted to wait. It was a good cause, after all.

On the bus home, the Prime Detectives sat together and discussed the weekend.

"So, Gabe is sleeping over at my house tonight," Cam said. "We'll be baking up a storm."

"*You'll* be baking up a storm," Gabe said. "*I'll* be checking your math."

"What are you doing tonight, Abby?" Cam asked.

"My parents and I are trying to figure out how to get General Humongulo to the fair," Abby said. "It will require some . . . effort."

"Ever heard of punkin' chunkin'?" Cam asked.

"*What-in what-in?*" Abby said.

"It's also known as pumpkin chucking, but *punkin' chunkin'* sounds so much better," Cam said. "It's where you build a catapult or a cannon to shoot pumpkins long distances. Maybe that's how you can get General Humongulo to the fair."

"Yeah, if I want to destroy the fair and crush multiple people!" Abby cried. "You don't realize how big this thing is."

"My grandpa has a front-end loader," Gabe said. "I'll ask him if he can drive it over for you. It's not a very long distance. I'm sure he'll say yes. But he'd probably want to do it at dawn before there's traffic on the roads."

"That'd be amazing," Abby said. "Thank you!"

"Could we maybe *punkin' chunk* it after the fair?" Cam asked. "Like in a big open field where no one will get crushed?"

"That seems like a waste," Abby said.

"But it would be cool," Cam said.

"He's right," Gabe said. "It would be."

Abby smiled and said, "We'll see. I've gotta win the contest first."

Abby had a very good shot at winning, too. She didn't know precisely how much General Humongulo weighed, but she did know a formula for getting a pumpkin's approximate weight. All she needed was three measurements.

MEASUREMENT 1: THE CIRCUMFERENCE

Circumference is the distance around a sphere. A sphere is a circle, but in three dimensions. A ball, basically. Or perhaps a planet, like Earth. The circumference of Earth is 24,901 miles at the equator. This means that if a person could walk in a straight line around the equator, they would have to travel 24,901 miles if they wanted to return to the

point where they started. For a perfect sphere, this measurement is the same no matter which way you walk. But Earth isn't a perfect sphere. It's a bit wider at the equator. The circumference around the poles, for instance, is forty-one miles smaller, at 24,860 miles. The world's biggest shortcut.

Pumpkins aren't perfect spheres, either. Especially big ones. They're lumpy and bulbous, with certain sides that are almost always flat. So, when measuring the circumference of a pumpkin, it's standard to measure around the widest part.

1. CIRCUMFERENCE

MEASUREMENT 2: THE HEIGHT

Pumpkin growers don't use a traditional measurement of height. Their measurement starts on the ground next to the stem of the pumpkin and reaches around the pumpkin to the ground next to the base, where the blossom once grew. Often, this is the longest side of the pumpkin.

2. HEIGHT

MEASUREMENT 3: THE WIDTH

Measurements of width are also a bit different with pumpkins. They start at the ground on one side of the pumpkin and reach around to the other side. Width will usually be shorter than height, but not always.

3. WIDTH

The dimensions for Abby's pumpkin, General Humongulo, were as follows:

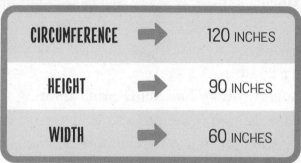

CIRCUMFERENCE	➡	120 INCHES
HEIGHT	➡	90 INCHES
WIDTH	➡	60 INCHES

When her calculations were added together, the result was known as the Over-the-Top Measurement, or the OTT.

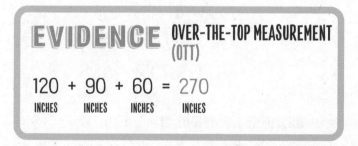

EVIDENCE OVER-THE-TOP MEASUREMENT (OTT)

120 + 90 + 60 = 270
INCHES INCHES INCHES INCHES

Abby knew that using the OTT in a very-hard-to-calculate formula would give her the approximate weight of her pumpkin.

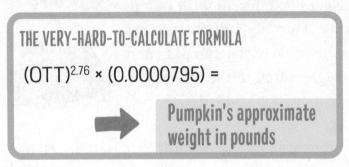

THE VERY-HARD-TO-CALCULATE FORMULA

$(OTT)^{2.76} \times (0.0000795) = $

Pumpkin's approximate weight in pounds

Yikes.

It would be nearly impossible, even for Abby "the Abacus" Feldstein, to do such a calculation in her head.

Luckily, Abby had some programming skills. So, she created a simple app that would do the calculation for her. All she had to do was plug in the OTT and the app would tell her approximately how much a pumpkin weighed. In the case of General Humongulo, the result was four hundred eight pounds.

SOLVED OTT = 270 INCHES

$270^{2.76} \times (0.0000795) = 408$
OTT   POUNDS

approximate weight of 408 pounds

That's one big pumpkin!

"General Humongulo has a lift to the fair," Abby announced shortly after she arrived home that afternoon.

"'A lift?'" her dad asked as he looked up from a novel he was reading.

"On Gabe's front-end loader," Abby said as she petted her three cats. First Boogie, then Bumpus, and finally Doug.

"Little Gabe has a front-end loader?" her mom said as she peered around a canvas she was painting.

"His grandfather does," Abby told her. "Gabe just sent me a message. His grandfather said he's happy to do it. The machine should be here first thing in the morning, so we better get our champion ready."

Getting General Humongulo ready involved painting a giant snarling face on his broad side and then topping him with a small green plastic wading pool, to make it look like he was wearing a military helmet.

So that's what Abby and her parents spent the afternoon and evening doing. Abby told her mom how she wanted General Humongulo to look. Abby's mom was an artist, so she did the painting. Abby's dad was an English professor, so he . . . critiqued the painting. Thankfully, they all thought it was a masterpiece.

Meanwhile, Cam and Gabe spent the afternoon and evening in Cam's crowded kitchen. It was crowded because Cam's three sisters—Toni, Kelly, and Raquel—were in the kitchen, too. The boys were mixing flour, butter, salt, sugar, and water to make pie dough. The girls were peeling and cutting apples. And Cam was the only one who was particularly happy about it.

"My sisters and my best chum, all pitching in," he said. "This is the definition of fun."

Gabe groaned and pointed down at his powdery shirt. "I'm covered in flour. I didn't sign up for this."

"I told you to wear an apron," Cam said.

"You mean this one?" Gabe said, grabbing a ridiculous, frilly little thing with the words MOMMY'S LIL' COOK on it.

Cam shrugged, kneaded a big ball of dough, and said, "It's one of my favorites."

At the other side of the kitchen, Toni let out a loud sigh.

"I'd rather be wearing *that* than doing *this*," she said as she held up a long, thin apple peel. Then she tossed it over her shoulder onto a mountain of apple peels that had collected on the counter.

"How many apples are we peeling again?" Kelly asked.

"We're cooking twenty-one pies, and we need eight apples per pie," Cam said.

"So, a million, basically?" Raquel asked.

"Or one hundred sixty-eight," Cam said. "Which is twenty-one multiplied by eight."

Gabe patted Cam on the shoulder, which caused a cloud of flour to puff into the air. "That was a quick calculation, buddy," Gabe said. "We've taught you well."

Cam smiled proudly, but his sister Toni groaned.

"I'm not peeling one hundred sixty-eight apples," she said.

"Don't worry," Gabe told her. "You only have to peel fifty-six. Because there's three of you and one hundred sixty-eight divided by three is fifty-six."

"Fifty-six is still a lot," Kelly said.

"True, but remember," Cam said, "one of those twenty-one apple pies will be all yours."

The three sisters thought about the arrangement for a moment. They obviously knew what everyone else in their family knew: Cam was an amazing chef. Plus, with the assistance of friends like Gabe, who was teaching him to be better at measurements and calculations, Cam was becoming an amazing baker, too. So amazing, in fact, that he was scheduled to appear on a game show called *Triumph or Caketastrophe*.

Triumph or Caketastrophe was the world's only televised baking and obstacle course competition featuring children between the ages of nine and twelve. Cam's appearance was still a few months away, but he was determined to win. And while his sisters certainly liked to tease him, Toni, Kelly, and Raquel were also determined to help him win. Baking these twenty-one pies for the fall festival was practice, and delicious practice at that.

"It's worth it," Raquel finally said. Her two sisters sighed and nodded. They all got back to peeling.

Chapter 5

A ROLLING WHEEL
OF TICKETS

When the sun rose the next morning, General Humongulo glistened with dew. Gabe's grandfather arrived and scooped the giant pumpkin onto his front-end loader. Abby and her parents waved as the vehicle pulled away. Then they got ready for the big day.

Down the street at Cam's house, the pies that had been cooked the night before had cooled down enough that Cam and Gabe could load them into boxes. They carried twenty boxes to the family's SUV and lowered the seats so they could fill the entire back. Then Cam's mom kissed him on the cheek, told him she was proud of him, and drove the pies to the fair. One pie stayed at home on the kitchen counter, as a payment to his sisters. It was already half eaten.

Abby's parents drove Abby, Cam, and Gabe to the fair, and the back seat was abuzz with talk of the future.

"What will you do when you win?" Gabe asked.

"Are you talking about me?" Abby and Cam said at the same time.

"Both of you," Gabe said. "You're both going to win."

"I'll simply be elated," Cam said. "Knowing people enjoyed my pies will be a big enough reward for me. As will eating that pie in the pie-eating contest."

"I'm looking forward to the *real* prize," Abby said.

"You get to meet a real black rhino, right?" Gabe asked.

"Yep," Abby said. "Ricky has promised a private tour of the wildlife sanctuary for all the contest winners. We'll get to see all the local animals they've saved. Plus, we'll get a close-up view of an actual black rhino. So, it will be a real treat to see where all the money is going."

"I don't remember if I already asked, but do you get to bring a guest?" Gabe said with his eyebrows raised.

"You have already asked," Cam said. "Many times."

"And the answer is . . ." Abby paused for dramatic effect. Then she punched Gabe playfully on the shoulder. "Of course one of us will bring you. Can't divide the Prime Detectives, after all. Who knows? Maybe there will be a mystery we need to solve there."

"Or maybe there's a mystery we need to solve here," Cam said, and he pointed out the window.

The car had arrived at the fall festival, and things appeared to be in disarray. A crowd of kids had gathered near the ticket booth at the entrance, and many of them were gesturing wildly and shouting.

"Dad, can you drop us off here before you park the car?" Abby asked. "We should probably check this out."

Abby's dad pulled to a stop, and the three kids tumbled out of the car and raced into the throng.

"What's going on?" Cam asked.

"There are no tickets left," Noah told him. "Everyone has money to pay, but the tickets are gone."

"You mean someone already bought them all?" Abby asked.

"Nope," Noah said. "I mean they disappeared."

"Stolen?" Gabe asked.

Noah shrugged. "Go ask at the booth."

There was only one person behind the ticket booth, but it was difficult to see who it was because of all the other people in the way. Luckily Gabe was small. His size was rarely an advantage when he was playing sports, but it was an advantage now. He squeezed himself through the crowd and wiggled his way to the front. That's where he came face-to-face with Maisie. Hunched over behind the booth, with her head in her hands, she was quite clearly upset.

"I'm sorry, I'm sorry, I'm sorry," she told the angry kids. "I don't know what to do. Maybe we should just cancel the fair."

This seemed a bit extreme, so Gabe tapped her on the hand. "Come with me," he said, motioning with his chin away from the booth. "Maybe the Prime Detectives can help."

This seemed to calm her for a moment, and she announced, "Help is here. I'll be right back." She followed Gabe through the crowd until they reached a quiet spot where Abby and Cam were waiting.

"What happened?" Cam asked.

"It's simple," Maisie said. "When my sister, Haley, and I opened the booth this morning, the tickets were gone."

"Was the booth locked?" Gabe asked. "And who had access to it?"

"Everyone had access to it because there were only tickets inside," Maisie said. "We didn't think we'd need one."

"Where's Haley?" Abby asked.

"Trying to find the tickets, I think," Maisie said. "She rushed off and left me alone to deal with everyone."

"Why don't you create some new tickets right now?" Cam said. "We could help you. Get some paper and some scissors and draw some little symbols on them."

"But what about the tickets that were already sold yesterday and the ones that disappeared?" Maisie said. "We have to accept those, too, right? What if someone has the missing ones and they use them all without paying for them? So, the only fair thing to do is—"

"Found 'em!" a voice called out.

All heads turned from the booth toward the parking lot. There was Maisie's older sister, Haley, holding up a roll of tickets the size of a bicycle wheel. She waved it triumphantly.

Maisie's jaw dropped. "Where'd you find them?"

"I was walking back to the car when I spotted them under a bush," Haley said, pointing toward a line of shrubs at the edge of the parking lot. "Maybe they fell out of the booth and rolled over there."

Now Maisie's entire face dropped. "I feel like this is my fault in some way."

"I doubt it's anyone's fault," Haley said. "One of those things, you know. All that matters is that we have the tickets. So, it means we can start selling them. I think that'll make everyone happy."

She wasn't wrong.

A sunny attitude swept over the crowd as everyone scrambled to buy their tickets. The Prime Detectives pitched in, helping with the sales. In minutes, half the roll was gone. Gabe became a proud owner of ten tickets himself.

"So that was the easiest case we've ever solved," Cam said as soon as the line had thinned out and their help was no longer needed.

"I don't think we actually solved anything," Abby replied. "Haley solved it."

"We at least provided moral support," Cam said.

"I'm just happy that we can now go to"—Gabe paused to wave his ten tickets in the air like they were all winners—"the dunk tank!" He shouted the last part.

Then he was off into the thick of the festival. Cam was hot on his trail. But Abby paused for a moment. She stared across the parking lot to the line of shrubs where Haley had found the tickets. There was something else there.

Jogging over to the spot, she discovered that it was . . . trash? Or perhaps recycling. It was an empty can of black paint tipped over on its side and hidden behind some branches. When she lifted it by the handle, Abby noticed a word written on the can: DICEROS.

Was that Spanish?

She wasn't sure because she couldn't speak it.

But was the can of paint a clue?

Even if it was, Abby didn't want to lug it around all day. So, she left it there and put it in her memory palace instead. It was a technique she used to file away images and objects in her brain so she could remember them later. It involved  imagining a large building (a palace, for example) that housed all the things she wanted to remember. Later, when she wanted to access the memory, she simply closed her eyes and imagined walking through the building and coming across all the images and objects.

Usually, she had no reason to remember most things, and she thought that perhaps this time was no different. Still, it had become second nature for her, especially since she was part of a mystery-solving trio.

Speaking of which, Abby didn't want to be left behind. So, she took a deep breath and then she hurried into the fair after her friends.

Chapter 6

DUNK TANK TIME

The festival was in full swing. There were booths selling tasty apple treats and cider. Other booths offered carnival games and face painting. A bluegrass band played at one end of the field, while people competed in sack races at another end. And in the middle of it all was the one thing that so many of the fourth graders from Arithmos Elementary had come to see: the dunk tank!

This was a unique dunk tank, too. Instead of a target for a baseball that would trigger the trapdoor and drop the unfortunate person into the water, there was a lever rigged inside a basketball hoop. Kids would shoot basketballs at the hoop. If a shot went in, the trapdoor opened.

Easy, right? Only problem was that it was, by its very definition, a long shot. The kids had to stand behind a line that was a great distance from the hoop. But no one seemed to care about that. Everyone was too busy thinking about dunking Mrs. E.

Mrs. E. would be sitting in the dunk tank for exactly one hour. While the fourth graders adored their teacher, they wanted nothing more than to see her plunge into that water. She had egged them on, after all, joking about being "invincible." In fact, she had kept up with her boasting through the entire day on Friday. By Saturday morning, every kid in fourth grade, not to mention some of their brothers and sisters, wanted to take a shot at the dunk tank.

When Abby, Gabe, and Cam reached the tank, a line had already formed. Mrs. E. wasn't there yet, but she was supposed to arrive soon. It gave Gabe a moment to convince the crowd of something. There was a tree stump nearby, so he climbed onto it and placed his hands around his mouth to make his voice louder.

"Kids of Arithmos Elementary!" he cried. "Give me all your tickets!"

It was no surprise that the crowd exploded with laughter.

"I'm serious," Gabe went on. "Who here wants to see Mrs. E. get dunked over and over again?"

Instead of laughs, there were now cheers.

"Okay, then," Gabe said. "That's why you have to give me all your tickets. Right now!"

Now there were boos.

He waved his hands. "You won't boo when I tell you about the statistics!"

They continued to boo.

As good as he was at statistics, and math in general, Gabe wasn't always the best at convincing people. That's where Cam and Abby came in. They joined him on the tree stump.

"Please listen to Gabe," Cam told them. "And I say this as someone who sympathizes with you. Most of the time, I can't stand listening to Gabe."

"But this time you should definitely listen," Abby said. "Because I can assure you that his math on this is perfect."

The boos got quieter. Kids respected Gabe, but they really liked Cam, and they always trusted Abby. These two endorsements meant everything.

"I guess I should explain," Gabe said when it was quiet again. "*I'm* not going to spend your tickets. I'm going to give them to Luciana and Emmett."

"How is that any better?" Noah asked.

"Let's look at it this way," Gabe said. "Do you want Mrs. E. to be dunked two times? Or twenty times?"

"Twenty times, obviously," Kiko said.

"So, when we give all the tickets to Luciana and Emmett, that's what will happen," Gabe said. "Have a look at this."

Gabe pulled a folded piece of paper from his pocket. It didn't look very big at first, but then he unfolded it five times and it turned out to be as big as a poster. He held it in front of his body so everyone could see it. It was covered in equations, and he pointed to them as he spoke.

"There are twenty-five kids in line," he said. "I've been told that each kid has an average of two tickets to spend on the dunk booth. So that's fifty tickets total."

"Each ticket gives the kid four balls to shoot into the dunk tank hoop. So that's two hundred balls total to shoot."

"Does that sound like a lot of balls?" he asked.

"It sure does to me," Cam said.

"But would it surprise you to know that maybe none of those balls will dunk Mrs. E.?"

"That doesn't make any sense," Cam said.

"Sure, it does. Because most carnival games like this are a scam," Gabe said. "They're designed for the average person to lose. Have a look at this."

Gabe hopped down from the tree stump and walked over to a line that was spray-painted in the grass. Then he paced toward the basketball hoop connected to the dunk tank, counting out his steps—"One, two, three . . ."—until he was standing under the basket and had counted to ten.

"What does that mean?" Kiko asked.

"My pace is about two feet long," Gabe said. "That means the shot is from about twenty feet. That's basically a three-pointer. Even if they're lucky, the average fourth grader is not gonna hit a three-pointer."

"How do you know?" Grayson asked.

"He's been analyzing every kid's shooting ability for a while now," Cam said. "You're new this year, so he only has a month of data on you and your brothers."

"Which is more than enough," Gabe said.

"Sorry, but all three of you Penderton triplets should just hand over your tickets right now, because there's no way you're hitting that shot."

Mason grumbled and asked, "And what do you want to do with our tickets again?"

"Give them to Emmett and Luciana," Gabe said. "I've calculated that most of you have about a one-in-one-hundred chance of hitting the shot. So, most of you will have wasted your money. Because maybe only two of you will sink it. With those odds, it's possible that none of you will. Emmett and Luciana, on the other hand, are trained and skilled. They should be able to hit at least one out of ten shots. That's still not a great three-point shooting percentage, but it's excellent for a fourth grader. And with two hundred balls, that's at least twenty baskets. Possibly fewer, but probably more if they get in the zone."

$$\frac{1}{100} \times 200 = 2 \text{ (maybe fewer)}$$
BASKETS

$$\frac{1}{10} \times 200 = 20 \text{ (or more)}$$
BASKETS

"That's the math," Gabe went on. "And the math doesn't lie. So, you gotta ask yourself, how many times do you want to see Mrs. E. get dunked? Once, twice, maybe not at all? Or twenty times or more?"

All of a sudden, Mrs. E. appeared in the distance, wearing an orange swim dress with white lettering on it. She paced confidently toward the dunk tank, waving to the kids in line. When she got closer, it became easier to read the writing on the swim dress.

THE UNSINKABLE MRS. E.!

It didn't take the kids very long to make their decisions. They all quickly handed their tickets to Emmett and Luciana. Then they rubbed their hands in anticipation.

Luciana and Emmett stood side by side at the painted line in the grass, twenty feet from the dunk tank. Ten basketballs, painted like jack-o'-lanterns, sat on the ground next to them. Mrs. E. sat on the seat, which was also a trapdoor that hovered over the water. A group of kids stood near the dunk tank, ready to retrieve any balls that went astray. And Abby, Cam, and Gabe stood off to the side, next to an iPad that was mounted on a tripod. Mrs. E. had loaned them the iPad so they could record the event.

"I want proof that no one can dunk me," Mrs. E. had said with a laugh.

Abby hit record on the iPad and said, "We're rolling."

And Luciana and Emmett started shooting.

They alternated shots, with Luciana shooting right-handed and Emmett shooting left-handed.

"You got this!" Cam shouted.

Gabe raised a finger to his lips and shushed him. "Don't jinx them," he whispered. "Let them get focused first."

Cam blushed and quieted down.

Luciana and Emmett started alternating shots.

Miss. Miss.

Miss. Miss.

Miss. Miss.

Miss. Miss.

Miss. Miss.

They were out of balls. So, the other kids

quickly collected them. Cam turned to Gabe with a worried look, but Gabe shrugged it off. He knew if they were expected to hit one out of ten of their shots, then this was not surprising. Those first ten shots were simply a warm-up.

"You're going down, Mrs. E.!" Sanjeev shouted.

"You can't beat Gabe's rock-solid statistics!" Cam shouted.

This time, Gabe didn't shush them. The two seemed focused now, and he knew that having the crowd on their side could help. It was known as home field advantage. So, he even gave a supportive whistle while Emmett and Luciana let their shots fly.

Miss. Miss.

Miss. Miss.

Miss. Miss.

Miss. Miss.

Miss. Miss.

They were out of balls again. While the kids scrambled to pick them up, Mrs. E. playfully teased Emmett and Luciana.

"If I were you, I'd try aiming for the hoop," she called out.

This made Luciana shake her head and Emmett grumble something under his breath. It was clear she was getting to them.

"Just relax," Noah told Emmett and Luciana as he dropped a couple of balls next to their feet.

"We are relaxed," Luciana said.

"We're just unlucky," Emmett said.

"Actually, not that unlucky," Gabe said. "It's all still in the realm of statistics. You should sink one very soon."

With the balls collected, they started shooting again.

Miss. Miss.

Miss. Miss.

Miss. Miss.

Miss. Miss.

Miss. Miss.

"Um . . . when is soon?" Abby whispered. "They're hardly even hitting the backboard."

"Next ten shots," Gabe said. "I guarantee."

But there were ten more shots and ten more misses.

As the kids collected the balls, Mrs. E. called out, "You're zero for forty. If my calculation is correct, that's zero percent."

"Is her calculation correct?" Cam asked Gabe. Gabe gave him a look that said: *Are you kidding me?*

And things only got worse from there.

Soon it was 0–60, then 0–80, and 0–100.

Gabe knew that the top NBA shooters might take hundreds of three-point shots a day when they practiced. But as good as Luciana and Emmett were, they were kids. After fifty shots apiece, they were clearly slowing down. It only stood to reason that their shooting would get worse.

"We should've shot the balls ourselves," Kiko said.

Gabe was visibly shaken. Sweating. Stuttering. "It's . . . it's . . . it's fine. They'll go on a hot streak."

Emmett and Luciana didn't appear nearly as upset as he did. But they also didn't go on a hot streak. They were focused, but they were indeed slowing down. They continued to miss. Badly, too. Nearly every shot was an air ball.

0–120

0–140

0–160

0–180

"Zero for one hundred ninety-nine," Gabe whispered, shaking his head because he could hardly believe it. "And ten seconds to go before Mrs. E. has to leave."

"Last ball," Abby said, placing her hand on Gabe's shoulder.

Emmett shot.

Of course, Emmett missed.

"I'm sorry," Emmett said with a sigh.

"Me, too," Luciana whispered with guilt.

No one could blame them for what they did next. They both hightailed it out of there.

Meanwhile, Mrs. E. climbed down from the dunk tank, completely dry. She pointed to the words on her swimsuit—THE UNSINKABLE MRS. E.!—and said, "It isn't a lie, my friends. No lies detected. Catch you all later."

Then she strutted off into the fair.

That's when the crowd of kids descended on Gabe.

It was hard to hear anything over all the shouting, but Gabe could make out a few words and phrases.

"You tricked us!"

"Stolen!"

"Entirely unsinkable!"

Luciana and Emmett were long gone, so Gabe was the obvious scapegoat. Perhaps he should've been. He had convinced them to bet all their tickets on two people. And those bets had lost.

"Let me talk!" he cried, waving his hands in the air. "I can figure out what went wrong!"

It would be even harder to convince them of anything now. They kept shouting and getting up in Gabe's face. Abby and Cam waved their hands, too, but no one paid attention to them. They were equally guilty for endorsing Gabe's plan.

It wasn't until Maisie showed up that the crowd shifted their attention.

"I have a solution!" Maisie shouted.

Everyone turned to her.

"If it involves getting Mrs. E. back here and dunking her, we're all ears," Noah said.

"I'm not sure if I can do that," Maisie said. "But I can give you all your money back."

This silenced nearly everyone. Eyes darted back and forth. They were waiting to see who would be the first to take the offer.

"I mean, you should've been guaranteed at least a few dunks for all that money you spent," Maisie went on.

"That money is for Ricky's Rhinos," Abby said. "We can't take it back."

Other kids started nodding and agreeing, even though it was probably tempting to ask for their money back.

"I have a solution," Gabe said.

"Oh great," Sanjeev said with a groan. "Here we go again."

"I think you'll like this solution," Gabe said. "But first I have to ask Cam and Abby to do something for me."

He motioned for them to join him, and they huddled up. After a bit of whispering, Abby and Cam nodded and then walked over and took Mrs. E.'s iPad off the tripod. At the same time, Gabe walked over to the dunk tank.

"There's no one scheduled to be in the dunk tank for at least another hour," Gabe said. "So why don't I get in the dunk tank?"

Eyes lit up. Heads nodded. Smiles bloomed.

"If Maisie is okay with it, you can all get back in line, and try to dunk me without buying any more tickets," Gabe said. "Ricky's Rhinos gets money, and you get your revenge."

No one objected. Maisie included. She shrugged and said, "Yeah. I guess that works."

Gabe accepted his fate with a solemn nod, and he climbed up onto the seat above the water. He wasn't wearing a swimsuit and he didn't have a towel, but he was willing to risk shivering and dampness. Time, and an investigation, would ultimately tell if he had actually made a mistake.

"So out of two hundred shots, how many are *supposed* to go in?" Noah asked as he picked up a basketball and tossed it to himself.

Gabe knew it was probably not wise to throw more statistics at them at this point. So, he simply shrugged and said, "Why don't you take a few shots, and we'll see."

Chapter 7

THE CASE OF THE WAYWARD BASKETBALLS

The statistics were accurate. Two hundred basketball shots resulted in two baskets and two dunks. The first basket came relatively early, on the twenty-fifth shot. Sanjeev lofted a ball that followed a high arc, bounced on the rim, and fell in. The crowd cheered as Gabe plunged into the water. The second basket came relatively late, on the one hundred sixty-ninth shot. Tossing the ball underhand, Kiko hit a perfect swish, and the crowd cheered even louder. Two dunks were good enough for them.

It was exactly as Gabe had predicted. And considering that both Sanjeev and Kiko had suffered through tough mornings the day before, it felt like a huge win. They walked away smiling. And Gabe walked away recharged . . . and damp.

He went directly to the pumpkin patch. It wasn't an actual pumpkin patch because no pumpkins were growing there. But it was the spot where all the pumpkins sat on pallets so that they could be weighed for the contest. When Gabe arrived, two things were immediately obvious.

One: The ground was muddy and covered in tire tracks.

Two: General Humongulo was humongous! The three other pumpkins in contention were almost as big, but Abby's pumpkin was clearly the biggest of the bunch.

"Wow," Gabe said. "He's grown a lot since I last saw him."

"Water and sunshine," Abby said. "Breakfast of champions."

Abby and Cam were sitting in camp chairs next to the pumpkin. Cam had Mrs. E.'s iPad in his lap. He looked up from it and said, "Looks like they dunked you real good."

"Twice," Gabe said. "Exactly as I had calculated. Which makes me even more confident that something strange was happening with Emmett and Luciana."

"I'll let you be the judge," Cam said. "We did what you asked. We marked every missed shot. Have a look."

Cam showed Gabe a sped-up version of the video of Mrs. E. and the dunk tank. Over the last hour, Cam and Abby had been editing the video. It was an easy edit. They sped the video up because Gabe wanted the edit to be done quickly, and there was a lot of unimportant footage of Emmett and Luciana preparing for their shots. All Gabe cared about was where the basketballs went.

So, Cam and Abby used a simple drawing tool to tap dots on the screen where each basketball missed the basket. That meant that by the end of the video, there were two hundred dots on the screen, showing where each shot went astray.

"Very interesting," Gabe said as he paused the video right after the last shot. "Do you notice what I notice?"

"I'm not sure," Cam said. "There are a lot of dots."

"We marked Luciana's shots with red dots and Emmett's with green dots," Abby said. "It looks like the red dots are mostly on the right side of the target and the green dots are on the left side of the target."

"Yeah, it does," Gabe said.

"Is that because Luciana is right-handed and Emmett is left-handed?" Cam asked.

"I had the same thought," Gabe said. "And watch this."

Gabe then used a drawing tool to outline the basketball hoop. Because of the perspective, it was oval shaped. The oval obviously didn't have any dots in it because Luciana and Emmett didn't make any of their shots. But when Gabe used the cursor to move the oval over to the right, a series of red dots representing Luciana's shots filled it.

"So, what are we seeing?" Cam asked.

"We're seeing that the shots were off target," Gabe said. "But they were also clumped together. Watch this."

Gabe outlined the hoop again. He moved it over to the left. The green dots that represented Emmett's shots filled this oval, too.

Abby quickly figured out what was happening, "It's almost as if . . . they weren't aiming at the hoop."

"Exactly," Gabe said. "Count the dots in the oval."

"They're so clumped together that it's a little hard to tell," Cam said. "But I'd guess there's at least ten dots in each oval."

"I'd guess the same," Gabe said. "So that's about twenty dots total in those two ovals. And how many shots did I say they might hit?"

"About twenty," Cam said.

"Which proves what Abby said," Gabe told him. "Luciana and Emmett weren't aiming at the hoop. They were aiming to the side of the hoop."

"Or maybe they were just unlucky," Cam said.

"They'd have to be the unluckiest kids in the world," Gabe told him. "And the math proves it."

"The math proves what?" a voice said.

The Prime Detectives looked up to find Mrs. E. standing next to them. She put out her hands.

The gesture was clear. She wanted her iPad back.

"Can we use it for a few more minutes?" Gabe asked. "I need to calculate something."

Mrs. E. nodded to Abby. "But Abby the Abacus is standing right there."

Abby blushed and said, "It's true."

"Yeah, but I always like to check her work," Gabe said.

Mrs. E. looked at Abby, and Abby shrugged. "Okay," Mrs. E. said. "Five minutes."

"That's all I need," Gabe said as he immediately began tapping the screen of the iPad to write down equations. "Cam wondered if Luciana and Emmett were just unlucky when it came to missing their target. As I said before, they had a shooting accuracy of about one out of ten. That means for every ten shots, they should've sunk one basket. That can be represented as the fraction one over ten, or one divided by ten."

EVIDENCE

$\frac{1}{10}$ or $1 \div 10$

"One divided by ten seems like a tricky equation," Cam said.

"It actually isn't," Gabe said. "Just look at it this way. What's one hundred divided by ten?"

"Ten," Cam said.

$$100 \div 10 \text{ or } {}^{100}\!/_{10} = 10$$

"Right. Easy. But what you have to realize is that all whole numbers have an invisible decimal point at the end of them. We just usually don't write it. But we could write it like this."

$$100. \div 10. = 10.$$

"Okay," Cam said. "So?"

"You'll notice that when we divided one hundred by ten, all we had to do was move the decimal point to the left one place to get our answer," Gabe said.

"Okay," Cam said.

"This is the same for any number divided by ten," Gabe said. "So, when we're dividing one by ten, we do the same thing. And you'll notice I added a zero so you could see the decimal point clearly in the answer."

$$1. \div 10. = 0.1$$

"Okay," Cam said. "So that means one divided by ten is one tenth, or zero point one?"

"Right," Gabe said. "But that number represents their ability to make a basket. I want to know how likely it would be for them to miss the basket."

"That would be nine out of ten, right?" Cam said. "Or nine divided by ten, which would be zero point nine."

$$9. \div 10. = 0.9$$

"You're learning fast!" Gabe said. "Looking at that number, it's obvious that Emmett and Luciana are more likely to miss their target than hit it. Nine times more likely, in fact, because one tenth times nine equals nine tenths, or zero point nine. But what is the likelihood that they would miss two hundred times in a row?"

"I don't even know how to begin to calculate that," Cam said.

"I do," Abby said. "You would have to raise nine tenths to the two hundredth power."

"What does that mean?" Cam said.

"It means you multiply nine tenths by itself two hundred times," Gabe said.

$$(9/10)^{200} \text{ or } 0.9 \times 0.9 \ldots$$

FOR 200 TIMES IN A ROW!

"That sounds hard," Cam said.

"It is hard," Gabe said. "But I bet Abby could at least do the first few powers of nine tenths in her head."

"Try me," Abby said.

So, Gabe said, "Well, the first power of nine tenths is—"

"Itself," Abby butted in to say. "Nine tenths. Or zero point nine."

$$0.9^1 = 0.9$$

"And the second power is zero point nine squared, which is?"

"Zero point eight one."

$$0.9^2 = 0.81$$

"That's nine times nine with the decimal place moved over two places, right?" Cam asked. "Right," Gabe said. "And the third power is zero point nine times zero point eight one, which is?"

"Zero point seven two nine," Abby said.

$$0.9^3 = 0.729$$

"Fourth power?" Gabe asked.
"Zero point six five six one," Abby said.

$$0.9^4 = 0.6561$$

"Fifth?"
"Zero point five nine zero four nine."

$$0.9^5 = 0.59049$$

"Sixth?"
"Zero point five three one four four one."

$$0.9^6 = 0.531441$$

"Okay, okay, I get it," Cam said. "Let's not

keep doing this forever. But I am noticing that you said you're raising the number to the two hundredth power, but the number is getting smaller."

"That's right," Gabe said. "Because when you multiply any number by a number that's less than one, it always results in a smaller number. Zero point nine is less than one, and that's what we're multiplying by."

"So what number is it when you raise zero point nine to the two hundredth power?" Cam asked Abby.

Abby shrugged and said, "That's beyond my powers of calculation."

"And where the iPad comes in," Gabe said as he tapped away. "According to this, zero point nine to the two hundredth power equals . . ."

He held it up for everyone to see.

$$0.9^{200} = 0.00000000070550791$$

"Whoa," Cam said. "That's a very small number. But what does it mean?"

"Remember we were trying to figure out the odds that Emmett and Luciana would miss all two hundred of their shots?" Gabe asked. "That very small number shows the odds. To turn it into a fraction we can understand better, all you have to do is put it over one."

$$0.00000000070550791/1.0$$

"The value of the fraction won't change if we move the decimal point," Gabe said. "Just as long as we move the decimal point the same number of places on both the top and bottom parts of the fraction."

"Is that right?" Cam asked.

Abby nodded and said, "The top number is called the numerator and the bottom number is called the denominator, and as long as you multiply or divide both by the same number, the value of the fraction will remain the same."

"So, when you're moving the decimal places one place to the left, it's like you're dividing the numerator and denominator both by ten," Gabe added.

"And moving it one spot to the right would be multiplying by ten?" Cam asked.

"Exactly," Gabe said. "But in this case, we're going to multiply by ten billion, because that will move the decimal point over ten spaces to the right and give us a fraction that's easier to understand. Approximately seven in ten billion."

"Really?" Cam said with a gasp. "Seven in ten billion?"

"Which is less likely than one in one billion," Gabe said.

"It's one in one billion, four hundred twenty-eight million, five hundred seventy-one thousand, four hundred twenty-eight point five seven, to be precise," Abby said.

"We'll take your word for it," Gabe said. "The point is, the odds that Luciana and Emmett would miss two hundred shots in a row are so small that it's basically impossible. Which means . . ."

"They missed on purpose," Cam said.

"You bet they did," Gabe said, and he turned to look at Mrs. E. She had been standing there, silently watching her students figure the equations out.

"Three things," Mrs. E. said. "Number one: I want to congratulate all three of you on some excellent math. Really fantastic stuff."

"Thank you," Abby said.

"You're welcome," Mrs. E. said. "Two: I'd like to assure you that I have no idea why Emmett and Luciana would've missed so many shots. I was actually hoping they'd hit a few baskets. It would've been a lot more fun for everyone. Myself included."

Gabe nodded and said, "I'm not going to make any accusations. But you're also not off the hook, Mrs. E."

This made Mrs. E. chuckle, and then she put out her hands and said, "Fair enough. But now we've gotten to number three. Which is this: I need my iPad back."

Gabe grumbled and handed it over.

Chapter 8

PIES, PIES, PIES

The Prime Detectives hustled their way through the fair. Cam insisted that they check on his apple pies before doing anything else. When they arrived at his booth, they were happy to see that ten pies had already been eaten. Cam's parents were busy dishing out the slices. They had agreed to keep a watch on the booth so that Cam could enjoy the fair with his friends.

"People are loving it," Cam's mom said. "Some are even coming back for seconds."

"I've had three slices myself!" his dad said.

"Save some for the judges!" Cam hollered.

The judges were, of course, anyone at the fair who sampled a slice of pie. Each booth competing in the pie-baking competition sold small slices for one ticket apiece. The slices came on paper plates. The plates at each booth were a different color. So, when people wanted to vote for their favorite pie, all they had to do was drop a colored plate into a large bin near the entrance to the fair. At the end of the festivities, the organizers planned to count the plates by color and declare a winner.

Cam held up one of his pie plates, which was green, and waved it in the direction of Gabe and Abby. "So, are you going to vote for my pie now or what?" he asked.

"I haven't tried any of the other pies yet," Gabe said matter-of-factly.

"We should definitely try them all before voting," Abby added.

Cam recoiled in horror. "You mean you might not vote for *my* pie?"

"I'll definitely consider voting for it," Abby said as she handed a ticket to Cam's mom. "One slice, please."

Cam's mom passed Abby a slice. Abby eyed it. She sniffed it. And then she put a fork to it. Taking a deep breath and clutching his hands up to his chest, Cam watched nervously as his friend ate the slice in three quick and uniform bites.

"Mmmm," Abby said. "Definitely a contender." Then she winked at Cam.

Cam exhaled. He turned to Gabe. He didn't need to say anything. It was clear what he wanted.

"You know I've already tasted it, but whatever," Gabe said, and he handed a ticket over and grabbed a slice. He ate his in a single bite and pocketed his green paper plate.

"Wow, Gabe," Abby said. "Maybe *you* should be entering the pie-eating contest."

"Speaking of which, it's about to start and I can't be late," Cam said. "We can worry about voting, and what happened at the dunk tank, later. It's time to EAT!"

Like the winner of the pumpkin-growing contest, the winner of the pie-eating contest would get to meet a black rhino at the local wildlife sanctuary where Maisie's uncle Ricky worked. Cam was excited for the prize. But mostly he was excited for the pies.

Because they were cherry pies. Having spent so long taste-testing apple pies, Cam was thrilled to sample something different. And since he hadn't eaten breakfast that morning, he was plenty hungry. To win the contest, he simply had to eat one cherry pie faster than the eight other contestants. Cam figured it would be easy . . . until he spotted the competition.

All the Penderton triplets (Jason, Mason, and Grayson) were entered, and Cam wasn't too worried about them. The five other contestants, however, were high school students. Not only that, but they were high school football players.

"Uh-oh," Gabe said. "That's the offensive line."

"What's offensive about them?" Abby asked. "They look like perfectly nice guys."

Gabe rolled his eyes. "They *are* perfectly nice. I know them well. I do the statistics for the football team, in case you haven't heard."

Now it was Cam who rolled his eyes. "We know. You're the only fourth grader I've ever heard of who prints copies of his résumé and hands them out to random people at sporting events."

Gabe shrugged it off. "Never know when there might be another statistician job on the horizon. But that's not important now. What's important is that all five offensive linemen are competing in this pie-eating contest. They're not offensive people. That's the name of the position they play. And it's a position for the biggest, hungriest players on the team. In other words, the best pie-eaters around."

Cam gulped. "I thought it would only be other kids, like the Penderton triplets."

"I think they made the contest open to anyone

under the age of eighteen," Gabe said. "Even if they don't look like it, these guys qualify."

The football players were all having a fantastic time, playfully teasing, and pushing each other, and saying things like "I'm gonna inhale that pie" and "Not if I smash it in your face first."

Abby chuckled. "They remind me of you two."

The football players looked happy, so in other circumstances Cam might've taken it as a compliment. But at the moment, Cam was feeling far from happy. He was feeling disappointed. This wasn't going to be an easy win like he'd thought.

"Not sure I have much of a chance versus

those guys," he said. "Each of them probably weighs three times as much as me."

"Sadly, that's true," Gabe said. "But we know you'll at least win the pie-baking competition. So, this is just for fun, right?"

"Yeah, and for lunch," Cam said. "I haven't eaten all day. Speaking of which . . . You shouldn't waste your time hanging out here waiting for me to get humiliated. If you want me to win the pie-baking competition, you two have to vote."

"Fair enough," Gabe said. "We'll get on it."

"After sampling the other pies, of course," Abby said.

"And after tracking down Emmett and Luciana," Gabe said. "We may have solved the mystery of the wayward basketballs, but we don't know their motive yet. Without a motive, it doesn't feel solved, does it?"

"True," Cam said. "So, go. And take your time. I'll let you know how badly I lose."

The Prime Detectives split up. Cam stayed behind to compete in the pie-eating contest. Gabe headed to one end of the fair, while Abby headed to the other. They were both searching for Emmett and Luciana while sampling the other entries in the pie-baking competition.

Abby's first stop was at the apple pie booth run by her piano teacher, Miss Lundegard.

"Hope it's a winner," Miss Lundegard said as she passed Abby a slice on an orange plate.

While Abby hoped it was tasty, she also hoped it wasn't nearly as good as Cam's pie. She liked Miss Lundegard. But she didn't need her decision to be a difficult one.

Thankfully, it wasn't going to be. Miss Lundegard's pie was awful. Way too sweet and far too soggy. Abby took a couple nibbles, and when she was sure Miss Lundegard wasn't looking, she hurried over to a nearby trash can and stuffed the orange plate inside.

She stuffed the plate inside because the trash can was overflowing. Which was strange. The fair had only opened a few hours before. There shouldn't have been enough trash already to fill the can. Unless, of course, everyone was throwing out the plates from Miss Lundegard's pie.

That wasn't the case, though. The trash can was indeed full of something orange, but it wasn't orange plates. It was empty boxes of orange . . .

"Jell-O?" Abby whispered to herself.

There must have been dozens of empty boxes of orange Jell-O in the trash can. Abby used a stick to sift through it all. They seemed to fill the entire thing. She snatched one of the boxes from the top. It felt like evidence . . . of something.

"Whatcha got there?" a voice asked.

Abby quickly slid the box into the pocket of her vest and turned to find Luciana standing there, staring at her.

"Oh . . . nothing," Abby said.

This seemed to satisfy Luciana, or at least didn't distract her from the other things on her mind. "I need to ask you something," she said to Abby.

"I need to ask you something, too," Abby replied. "You go first, though."

"Is everyone mad at me?" Luciana said.

Abby couldn't speak for everyone, so she said, "I know some people are disappointed."

"Can you tell those people that I didn't sleep very well last night?" Luciana said. "And that's why my aim was off."

"But that would be a lie," Abby said.

Luciana pulled her hands to her chest, as if she was protecting herself, and she whispered, "But how do you know that?"

"I don't know how you slept," Abby said. "But I do know how you shot those basketballs. They went exactly where you were aiming. Problem was, you weren't aiming at the hoop. The math tells us that."

Luciana lowered her head. She sighed like she had been defeated, probably because she knew that Abby's math was always indisputable. Finally, she said, "I'm sorry. But I did it for a good reason."

"Because you didn't want Mrs. E. to get dunked?"

Luciana shook her head. "Because Emmett told me to. He said if we missed all our shots, then it would mean everyone would buy more tickets and Ricky's Rhinos would get more money. I did it to help the cause."

"But that's not what happened, right?"

"I guess not."

"So, why did Emmett think it would work?"

"I don't know," Luciana said. "You'll have to ask him."

"We'd have to find him first," Abby said. "Maybe Gabe is having some luck in that department."

Gabe was having no luck in that department. He hadn't found Emmett. He had, however, found some more apple pie. He tried three other entries in the competition, and none held a candle to Cam's slices. Even though there were a few more entries to try, Gabe was confident that Cam had his vote. So, he decided he might as well drop Cam's green plate in the bin by the entrance.

As he made his way across the fair, he noticed a lemonade stand and thought he might buy a cup to wash down all that pie. Their art teacher, Miss Pelican, oversaw the stand, and as soon as

Gabe reached it, she hung a sign over the front that said CLOSED.

"Really?" Gabe asked. "The fair isn't over for a while."

Miss Pelican threw up her hands. "Yeah, but we're out of water. Someone emptied one of our containers."

She motioned to a large clear plastic container that was tipped over on its side.

"Who emptied it?" Gabe asked.

"Beats me," Miss Pelican said. "It was empty when we got here. Luckily, we had another, but we used it all up. We have to close shop for a bit while we track down some more water. There's no hose nearby, unfortunately."

Gabe peered over the edge of the booth at the ground. There was no grass. It was mostly dirt and gravel. But the ground was bone dry.

"Interesting," he whispered to himself as he turned away.

And that's when he saw something even more interesting.

Emmett!

He was buying a caramel apple from a booth in the distance. Gabe couldn't see him clearly, but he could see that when Emmett reached into his pocket to get a ticket to pay for the apple, something fell to the ground. Gabe raced toward him, weaving through the crowd. He moved as quickly as he could, but Gabe wasn't particularly fast or agile, and since he was short, he had trouble seeing past people. By the time he was at the caramel apple booth, Emmett was gone. But the thing Emmett dropped was still on the ground. Gabe snatched it up.

It was a smudged receipt. There was only one bit of text Gabe could make out.

That didn't mean anything to Gabe, and he sighed in disappointment. But the disappointment didn't last long. Because the receipt's paper was thin, and he could see that there was something written on the other side. Flipping it over, he read the following note, written in Magic Marker.

"Huh," Gabe said to himself as he examined the handwriting. He wasn't sure what he might discover from it. Handwriting was not his expertise. There was one person, however, who had an eye for such things.

He knew just where to find her.

Chapter 9

LISTEN, ALL Y'ALL, IT'S A SABOTAGE

The names of the pie-eating football players were Desmond, Sal, Manny, Conner, and Blake. Cam learned that because he was friendly and they were friendly and when their big hands shook his small hand, they introduced themselves.

"So, you think you're gonna beat us, little man?" Desmond asked.

Cam shrugged. "Probably not, but you never know."

"That's the spirit," Sal said. "When I was your age, I couldn't even eat half a pie."

"Yeah, you're a brave kid," Manny said.

"Or at least a hungry kid," Cam told him.

"You're friends with Gabe, right?" Conner asked.

"Friends and colleagues," Cam said.

Blake laughed. "So, you do statistics, too?"

"I'm learning," Cam said. "I know enough to know my odds aren't good today."

"Don't worry about the odds," Desmond said, and he patted Cam on the shoulder. "Only worry about your performance."

"Let's all worry about that," Sal said, motioning with his chin to the contest official. "Looks like we're about to start."

The contest official was the gym teacher, Mr. Largo. He pushed a cart with ten pies toward a long table. Then he set nine of the pies down on the table in front of nine chairs.

"Take your seats, gentlemen," Mr. Largo said.

The Penderton triplets sat first, then Cam, and then the football players. Cam leaned forward over his pie and gave it a sniff. He could sort of smell the crust, but not the cherry, which was a surprise. He had an excellent sense of smell. Perhaps he was coming down with a cold.

"The rules of the pie-eating contest are simple," Mr. Largo said. "No utensils. No hands. Eat until the plate is clean. If you feel sick, bow out. There's no shame in that. Any questions?"

"Where are all the girls?" someone shouted.

The participants looked at each other. But it

clearly wasn't one of them who said it. The voice came from the crowd. From Gabe's little sister, in fact. Emma was standing on a chair and shaking a fist.

"I said, 'Where are all the girls?'" Emma shouted again.

Mr. Largo stepped forward and answered. "That's a good question, Miss Kim. Where *are* all the girls? The contest was open to students in every school. But these are the only students who signed up. Would you like to join? I think we have another pie."

It gave Emma something to consider. She scratched her chin. She looked up at the clouds. Then she finally stepped down from the chair and sat on it. "No thanks. I prefer cake."

"Any other volunteers?" Mr. Largo asked.

There were no takers. But at that very moment, both Gabe and Abby arrived on the scene. Cam was thrilled to see them. He had assumed they were going to miss the contest.

They waved to Cam, and Gabe said something, but Cam couldn't hear it. From reading Gabe's lips, it seemed like he was saying, "Lose."

Lose? Really?

"I might not win," Cam shouted back. "But I'm not gonna lose."

Gabe put his hands over his eyes in embarrass-ment as Abby reached into her pocket and pulled out the empty Jell-O box.

"He said we have *CLUES*," she shouted.

That made more sense, and Cam flashed them a thumbs-up. There was nothing like fresh evidence to get his blood pumping. And his blood sure was pumping. He was almost ready. Just one last thing to do. To make room for all the pie he was going to eat, he reached down and loos-ened his belt by two notches.

Meanwhile, Mr. Largo raised his right hand, which was holding a stopwatch. "On your marks," he said.

All the participants put their hands behind their backs.

"Get set."

They leaned forward, mouths poised.

"And . . . eat!" Mr. Largo shouted as he thrust his hand down and started the stopwatch. The stopwatch might not have seemed necessary, because the main thing that mattered was who finished their pie first. That person would be declared the winner. But, at Gabe's request, Mr. Largo was keeping a record of the time. Wherever and whenever possible, Gabe gathered statistics. After all, he never knew when he might need to know how fast someone can eat a cherry pie.

Unfortunately, Gabe wouldn't have a chance to know that at all. Because as soon as the contestants' mouths hit the crusts of their pies, their heads popped back up again. Frustrated cries burst forth from the young men.

"I can't eat it!"

"It's too hard!"

"I think I broke a tooth!"

One of the Penderton triplets, Jason, took his pie and tipped it upside down while holding the aluminum dish. The pie fell out of the dish, but it didn't splatter or squoosh. It hit the table with a loud thud.

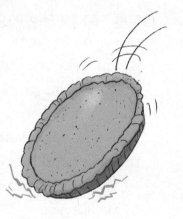

"They're frozen," Cam said, rapping his knuckles on his pie.

There were a few gasps from the crowd, Abby's the loudest of them all.

Mr. Largo set down the watch and picked up Jason's pie. He tapped it on the table—*tap, tap, tap*—and it stayed in one piece. "Huh," he said. "Frozen solid."

"We've been sabotaged!" Sal the football player cried.

"I bet it was Humanis High," Manny said.

"Yeah," Desmond said. "Probably trying to get revenge for our victory last night!"

"Whatever the reason, I think we have to declare that the pie-eating contest is over," Mr. Largo said. "Or at least postponed until these pies can defrost."

Still raring to go, Cam jumped from his seat and ran to the cart from which Mr. Largo had retrieved the pies. There was a single remaining pie on the cart, but also two other things. There was a large plastic funnel. And there was a metal apple corer, which was a cylindrical tube with a handle on one end and a serrated edge on the other end for cutting the cores out of apples.

Cam picked them up and brought them over to Mr. Largo.

"Are these yours?" he asked.

Mr. Largo shook his head. "Looks like things a baker might use. All this stuff was already here when I arrived this morning."

"Does anyone know who put this cart here?" Cam asked the crowd.

There were a lot of shrugs, but no good information. Frozen pies, a funnel, and an apple corer: That's all Cam had to work with. Still, they were clues, and a few clues was better than no clues. His friends motioned to him, and with the frozen pie, the funnel, and apple corer tucked under an arm, he headed toward them.

The Prime Detectives huddled together near a maple tree at the edge of the fair. They wanted privacy because it was hard to know who to trust.

"Something strange is afoot," Cam said.

"You said it," Abby replied.

"Let's go through all the bad things that have happened so far," Gabe said.

"The pies were frozen," Cam said.

"The dunk tank was rigged," Gabe said.

"And the tickets were missing," Abby said.

"It all points to the same objective," Gabe said. "Someone is trying to sabotage the fair."

"But who and why?" Abby said. "I'm not ready to make any accusations until we have more evidence."

"I have the receipt with the note," Gabe said. "Cam has the funnel and the apple corer. And you have that Jell-O box."

"Not sure what the Jell-O tells us," Abby said.

"It tells us someone has quite an appetite," Cam said.

"Let's get back to the receipt," Abby said. "Show it to us again."

Gabe revealed the receipt with the note on the back that read: *Thanks for the bad aim. You're an Awesomesaurus!*

"So, whoever wrote this convinced Emmett to miss all his shots, right?" Cam asked. "Who do you think wrote it?"

"Maybe I can tell you that," a voice said.

The voice wasn't a surprise this time because they all knew whose voice it was. It was Emma again. But at the moment, Emma was only a voice because she was hidden behind the red leaves of the maple tree. She had been climbing it while the others were discussing the sabotage scenario.

All of a sudden, Emma's feet poked out from the leaves, and then she dropped to the ground, landing with the grace of a cat. "Give it here," she said, motioning for the receipt.

Even at the age of eight, Emma was a talented artist, and she had an uncanny ability to identify who created certain works of art. Famous paintings by masters or simple drawings by her peers? It didn't matter. She could look at something and say, "That's clearly a Kandinsky," or "Obviously an Abby Feldstein."

The same talent translated to handwriting. So as soon as Gabe handed over the receipt, she gave it her full attention. Squinting at it, running her finger along the text, she studied it thoroughly. Then she delivered her evaluation.

"I have no idea who wrote this," she said.

"That's not much help," Gabe said.

"I can at least tell you some people who didn't write it," Emma said. "It wasn't any of you three. Or any of my friends. I don't think I've seen this person's handwriting before, so I can't know whose it might be."

"Can you tell whether a boy or a girl wrote it?" Cam asked.

"I'm not going to assign anyone a gender, thank you very much," Emma said.

"Do you at least know if it's a kid or an adult?" Abby asked.

Emma answered quickly, "Either a kid with good handwriting or an adult with somewhat sloppy handwriting. That would be my guess."

"Both of my parents have sloppy handwriting," Abby said.

"Do you think maybe . . . ?" Cam said softly.

Abby laughed. "What reason would my parents have to sabotage the fair?"

"Maybe they're making sure you're the only one who wins anything today," Gabe said.

"I think it's pretty clear that Cam will be winning the pie-baking competition," Abby said.

"Fingers crossed," Cam said.

"Are either of your parents left-handed?" Emma asked.

"No," Abby said. "Why?"

"Because whoever wrote this is left-handed," Emma said. "So, your parents are off the hook."

"Lemme see that," Gabe said as he grabbed

the receipt from her. "How do you know they're left-handed?"

"Sometimes you can see a smudge from left-handed writers because their hand runs over the ink as they write," Emma said. "I don't see that here. *Buuuut* . . . I can tell by the direction of the ink stroke that the top of the *T* was written from right to left, rather than left to right. See how the line starts with a dot and ends with a slash?"

"I hate to admit my sister is right, but yes, I see it," Gabe said. "And I think she's right."

"Typical left-handed handwriting," Emma said proudly.

"Can I have a look?" Cam asked, and Gabe passed him the receipt.

Cam examined the receipt. But instead of looking at the handwriting, he kept his eyes focused on the top corner. Those eyes went wide when he noticed something.

"Okay," Abby said. "So now that we've ruled my parents out as suspects, do we rule out all right-handers?"

"We can rule out anyone if we can get their fingerprints," Cam said. Then he held up the receipt, revealing a faint, but evident, black fingerprint on the corner.

If all the clues were a math equation, then it would've added up to nothing. At least for now. The Prime Detectives, joined by Emma, took all the clues with them as they left the maple tree and headed toward the pumpkin patch. The big event of the fair, the pumpkin weigh-in, was about to happen, and they didn't want to miss it.

When they reached the patch, they noticed that a forklift had arrived on the scene, along with a giant scale. Since all four pumpkins in the competition sat on wooden pallets, the forklift could easily lift them, carry them over to the scale, and set them down. Of course, to get that exact weight, the judges needed to subtract the weight of each pallet, which was forty pounds.

It would be a few minutes until the official weigh-in, enough time for the Prime Detectives to make sure nothing had gone awry. First, they spoke to Mr. Fritz, the third-grade teacher. He was in charge of driving the forklift and weighing the pumpkins.

"How's the scale doing?" Cam asked him. "Accurate enough to judge a winner?"

"Calibrated and tested to the ounce," Mr. Fritz said. "Good to go."

"Has anyone been tampering with anything?" Abby asked Mrs. Vernon. At school, Mrs. Vernon was the custodian. At the fair, she was the official pumpkin guard, and she stood with her arms crossed next to the pumpkin patch.

"Been pretty quiet all morning," Mrs. Vernon said. "Though lots of people have come by to admire the pumpkins."

The spectators had to stand at a distance, though, because the pumpkin patch was roped off. The only people allowed near the pumpkins were the people who grew them. Two of the other contestants stood next to their giant gourds with proud looks on their faces. One other pumpkin was all alone. No one stood next to it.

"Whose pumpkin is that?" Gabe asked Ms. Santiago, their school librarian, who was handling the record-keeping for the contest.

"Don't know," Ms. Santiago said. "It was the first one here this morning, before anyone else arrived. The paperwork was in order, though, so that's all that matters."

"Can we see the paperwork?" Cam asked. "Or is that . . . a violation of the pumpkin-grower's rights?"

Ms. Santiago laughed. "It's a pumpkin-growing contest, not a tax return. The paperwork is taped to the back. Have a look. Just don't touch."

The Prime Detectives circled around to the back of the lonely pumpkin, where sure enough, there was the paperwork.

ENTRANT NAME: Anonymous

PUMPKIN NAME: Mr. Jiggles

CONTACT INFORMATION: If I win, I will decline the prize. Winning is good enough for me.

That was it.

"That's not much help," Cam said.

"Sure, it is," Emma said, holding the receipt next to the paper. "Because the handwriting matches. Same left hand."

"Any black fingerprints?" Gabe asked.

Before they could examine it closer, Mrs. Vernon told them to move out of the way. Mr. Fritz was on the forklift, and he was driving over to pick up Mr. Jiggles. So, the kids made their way back to General Humongulo, and they removed his swimming pool helmet to prepare him for his official weigh-in.

"Who do you think grew Mr. Jiggles?" Cam said.

"Obviously the same person who wrote the note on the receipt," Gabe said.

"And who is that?"

"Probably Noah," Abby said.

This was a sudden and surprising accusation. One that had seemingly come out of nowhere. But Abby was saying it, so it had to come from somewhere.

"How do you know it's Noah?" Gabe asked.

"Yeah, what math did you use to figure it out?" Cam asked.

"Geometry?" Gabe asked.

"Algebra?" Cam asked.

"Calculus?" Emma asked.

"None of those things," Abby said. "Cam found a black fingerprint on the receipt, right?"

"Right," Gabe said.

Abby pointed into the distance and said, "I simply noticed that Noah has black paint on his hands."

They all peered around General Humongulo to see Noah standing in the crowd, his hands dangling at his sides. They were clearly jet black.

Gabe, who wasn't going to let another suspect

slip away, turned to Cam and said, "You know what to do. *Triumph or Caketastrophe.* Exactly like we trained."

That's all it took to rev Cam's engine back up. In a flash, he was off.

Cam chased Noah. And Noah ran.

For weeks, Cam had been training for his appearance on the game show *Triumph or Caketastrophe.* Yes, he was baking. But he was also running, jumping, and weaving. Why? Because *Triumph or Caketastrophe* was more than a baking competition.

To win, the young competitors would have to choose the ingredients for their cake, then carry those ingredients through an obstacle course without dropping them. Any ingredients they dropped, they couldn't use. After baking their cake, they'd have to carry it back through the obstacle course and present whatever remained to the judges.

Before his training had begun, Cam could barely run ten yards without doubling over to catch his breath. But Gabe had been coaching him. And while Cam wasn't the fastest kid around, he was now nimble, and negotiating a crowd was easy for him compared to the obstacles he had been mastering.

So, no matter how hard Noah tried to get away, Cam was hot on his trail.

Noah paused whenever someone stepped in his way, while Cam spun and dodged people.

Noah carefully climbed over a short plastic fence, while Cam leaped it at full speed.

Noah crawled under some low-hanging branches, while Cam rolled to keep up his momentum.

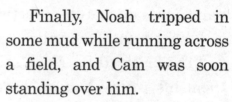

Finally, Noah tripped in some mud while running across a field, and Cam was soon standing over him.

"It wasn't me!" Noah screamed from the ground, hiding his hands behind his back. "It wasn't me! Please, don't blame it on me."

"What wasn't you?" Cam asked. "The note or the pumpkin?"

"The pie," Noah said. "I voted for your pie. It was delicious and I wanted you to win."

"Ooookay," Cam said.

That's when the other Prime Detectives arrived. First Abby, then Gabe.

"I know how this might look," Noah said. "But it's not the case."

"Why'd you write the note?" Gabe asked.

And Noah acted confused. "What note?"

"What's going on with Mr. Jiggles?" Abby said.

And Noah acted even more confused. "Who's he?"

"Why are your hands black?" Cam asked.

And Noah finally had an answer. "From the paint," he said matter-of-factly.

"What paint?" they all asked.

"The black stuff," Noah said, and he showed them his painty hands. "From the voting bin. But I didn't put it there. I just touched it."

"Wait, wait, wait," Gabe said. "Start over. Tell us what happened."

Noah finally took a deep breath, collected himself, and said, "I was going to vote for Cam's pie to win the pie-baking competition. So, I brought a green plate to the voting bin and dropped it through the slot in the lid.

At least I thought it was a green plate. I realized right away that I dropped the wrong plate in. Because the green plate was still in my hand! So, I stuck my hands down through the slot and inside the bin to pull out the wrong plate. That's when I felt something wet. I pulled my hands out, and they were covered in black paint. So, I opened the lid of the bin and saw that it was filled with black paint. All the plates had sunk into the paint. It was impossible to tell which color was which. It was all black. I came over to the pumpkin patch to find you guys and tell you, but when Cam started chasing me, I got scared. I probably shouldn't have run."

"That's all right," Cam said. "I needed the workout. So, what you're saying is someone messed up the pie-baking competition?"

"Seems that way," Noah said. "I'm sorry."

"Sounds like more sabotage," Abby said.

"At least you'll still win the pumpkin-growing contest," Gabe said to her.

Of course, he spoke too soon. Because at that moment, Emma joined them. She had run all the way from the pumpkin patch to deliver some news.

"Abby lost the pumpkin-growing contest," Emma said.

Chapter 10

THE SUSPICIOUS MR. JIGGLES

Abby didn't technically lose the pumpkin-growing contest. Her pumpkin, General Humongulo, came close, but not close enough. However, there was no prize for second place, so it might as well have been a loss.

The winner, of course, was Mr. Jiggles, the lonely pumpkin with the anonymous left-handed owner. When the Prime Detectives arrived back at the pumpkin patch, it had a large blue ribbon taped to its front.

On a nearby chalk-board, Ms. Santiago had listed the weights of the pumpkins.

PLUMPKIN: 282 pounds

ORANGE JULIUS: 306 pounds

GENERAL HUMONGULO: 413 pounds

MR. JIGGLES: 430 pounds (WINNER!)

"I can't believe we missed the weigh-in," Cam said. "I'm so sorry, Abby."

"Investigations always come first," Abby said firmly.

"And now we have to investigate how Mr. Jiggles won," Gabe said. "Because that's not possible. Something went wrong."

"Sorry to say it, but I watched the weigh-in and it was perfectly fair," Emma said. "The fork-lift picked each pumpkin up, placed it on the scale, picked it back up, and then put it back down. No one else was anywhere even close to the pumpkins or the scale."

"Did they maybe forget to subtract the weight of the pallet for Mr. Jiggles?" Cam asked.

"Nope," Emma said. "They did the calculations in front of everyone. It was all fair."

"And yet it doesn't seem fair, does it?" Abby said. "I need to do something about it. Cam, give me your belt."

Cam's eyes went wide. "But that's what holds my trousers up!"

"Did he just call his pants his *trousers*?" Emma asked.

"Don't worry," Gabe said. "Cam has an *interesting* vocabulary. I'm more concerned about why Abby would need his belt. What on earth do you plan to do with it?"

Abby laughed and said, "Well, obviously I'm going to use his belt to weigh all these pumpkins."

"Well, that makes *a whole lot* more sense," Emma said under her breath.

"Trust her," Gabe said. "She knows what she's doing."

Abby nodded to Cam, and Cam sighed and removed his belt. It was simply another sacrifice he would make for the sake of math. "I guess I'll hold my trousers up with my hands like a beltless fool," he said as he wrapped his fingers in the belt loops.

"This won't take long," Abby said, and she immediately carried the belt over to General Humongulo. Holding it like a tailor with a measuring tape, she stretched the belt along the circumference, the height, and the width of the pumpkin. When she came back, she announced her findings.

"General Humongulo is four belts around, three belts high, and two belts wide," Abby said.

"How does that help us?" Cam asked.

"Good question," Abby said, and she tore the paperwork off the back of her pumpkin. "I measured General Humongulo yesterday and used those measurements to figure out his approximate weight. I wrote all the numbers on the back here."

She showed everyone the other side of the paperwork.

EVIDENCE

GENERAL HUMONGULO'S MEASUREMENTS

CIRCUMFERENCE	HEIGHT	WIDTH
120	90	60
INCHES	INCHES	INCHES

> **OVER-THE-TOP (OTT) MEASUREMENT = CIRCUMFERENCE + HEIGHT + WIDTH**
>
> OTT=120 + 90 +60 = 270
>
> INCHES

> **(OTT TO THE POWER OF 2.76) × 0.0000795 = ESTIMATED WEIGHT**
>
> $(270^{2.76}) \times 0.0000795 = 408.254629043$
>
> ESTIMATED WEIGHT: **408** POUNDS

"Two hundred seventy to the power of two point seven six? Is that really a thing?" Gabe asked, because he knew a lot of math, but that seemed ridiculous even to him.

"It is a thing," Abby said. "The formula was figured out by some very smart pumpkin farmers. And no, I can't do the calculation in my head. But I did create an app to do the calculation. So now we can estimate the weight of the other pumpkins and see how close they match up to the real weights."

"But we don't have anything to measure them," Cam said.

Abby held the belt back up and shook it. "Like I said, my pumpkin is four belts around, three belts high, and two belts wide."

Cam slapped his forehead and said, "Right."

"So that means the belt is thirty inches long," Gabe said.

"Right!" Cam said again. "Because if you divide the original measurements by the number of belts, you get the length of the belt!"

Gabe pulled out his statistics notebook and wrote down the equations.

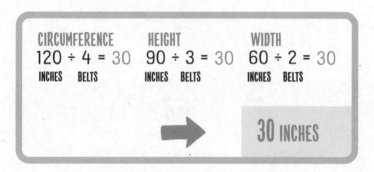

CIRCUMFERENCE
$120 \div 4 = 30$
INCHES   BELTS

HEIGHT
$90 \div 3 = 30$
INCHES   BELTS

WIDTH
$60 \div 2 = 30$
INCHES   BELTS

➡️ **30 INCHES**

"I don't know why you guys even need me around," Abby said. "You'd be fine on your own."

Emma shook her head firmly. "No, they wouldn't. They'd be a mess."

"I'm afraid my sister is right again," Gabe said with a sigh. "We all need you, Abs."

All of a sudden, Cam grabbed the belt from Abby and said, "And I need this. I'm gonna go measure the others."

No one stopped him. The contest was already over, so there was no reason to object to a boy holding his belt up to some pumpkins. Especially when he got to Mr. Jiggles. The pumpkin had been declared the winner, but there was still no one there to claim the prize.

Cam called out his measurements to Gabe, and he wrote them all down. When he was finished, they reviewed the details.

PLUMPKIN

CIRCUMFERENCE	HEIGHT	WIDTH
3 1/3	2 1/2	2
BELTS	BELTS	BELTS

ORANGE JULIUS

CIRCUMFERENCE	HEIGHT	WIDTH
3	1 2/3	3 1/2
BELTS	BELTS	BELTS

MR. JIGGLES

CIRCUMFERENCE	HEIGHT	WIDTH
3 ½	2 ⅓	3
BELTS	BELTS	BELTS

"How did you calculate halves and thirds of the belt?" Emma asked. "It doesn't have marks like a ruler."

Cam held the belt up and said, "Easy."

Then he easily folded it in half, then in thirds.

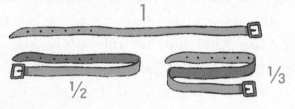

"Clever," Emma said.

Meanwhile, Abby reviewed the numbers. "So, there are a few ways we can convert this and use the numbers in my formula," she said. "Since you've been working on your conversions, Cam, why don't you give it a shot?"

"Sure," Cam said. "I'd start by converting all the measurements to inches. We know the belt is thirty inches. So, for Plumpkin, I'd multiply thirty inches by the number of belts in the circumference, height, and width."

"Do it," Abby said.

"The circumference is three and one third belts," Cam said. "So, I need to multiply thirty inches by three and one third. It might be easier to split the equation up into thirty times three plus thirty times one third."

"That works," Abby said.

"How does it work, though?" Emma asked. "You can't just break up math problems like that, can you?"

"You can always add two numbers together and then multiply them by another number," Abby said. "Or you can multiply those two numbers by the other number separately, and then add up the products. The answer is the same no matter which way you do it. It's called the distributive property."

"I don't care what it's called," Cam said. "I just know that thirty times three is ninety. But what's thirty times one third?"

Cam grabbed Gabe's notebook and wrote the equations large so everyone could follow along.

$$30 \times 3\tfrac{1}{3}$$
INCHES BELTS

$$(30 \times 3) + (30 \times \tfrac{1}{3}) = ?$$
$$30 \times 3 = 90$$
$$30 \times \tfrac{1}{3} = ?$$

"Thirty times one third is the same as thirty divided by three," Gabo said. "Think of it this way. Every whole number can be turned into a fraction. Simply put that number over one. So, thirty equals thirty over one."

Gabe took the notebook back and jotted down what he said.

$$30 = \frac{30}{1}$$

Cam nodded and Gabe went on. "And if you're going to multiply two fractions, you must multiply the two top numbers and the two bottom numbers. So, thirty over one times one over three is thirty times one over one times three. Or thirty over three."

$$\frac{30}{1} \times \frac{1}{3} = \frac{30 \times 1}{1 \times 3} = \frac{30}{3}$$

➡ Therefore ... $\frac{30}{1} \times \frac{1}{3} = 30 \div 3$

"Oh yeah," Cam said. "And thirty over three is basically a division equation. It's thirty divided by three. Which is ten, of course."

Cam took the notebook back and jotted it down.

$$30 \div 3 = 10$$

"So, I add ninety plus ten and I get one hundred inches for the circumference of Plumpkin."

Cam kept writing the equations as he worked through them.

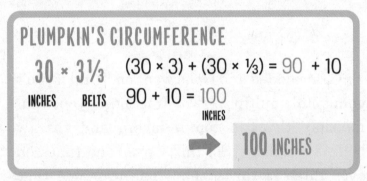

PLUMPKIN'S CIRCUMFERENCE

$30 \times 3\frac{1}{3}$

INCHES   BELTS

$(30 \times 3) + (30 \times \frac{1}{3}) = 90 + 10$

$90 + 10 = 100$
                    INCHES

➡ 100 INCHES

"How about the height?" Abby asked.

"Same method," Cam said. "The height is two and a half belts, so I multiply thirty by two, which is sixty. Then I multiply thirty by one half, which is the same as thirty divided by two. That's fifteen. Add sixty and fifteen together and I get a height of seventy-five inches."

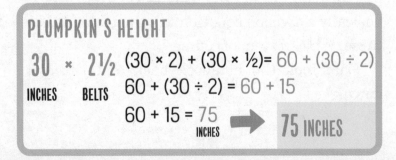

PLUMPKIN'S HEIGHT

$30 \times 2\frac{1}{2}$

INCHES   BELTS

$(30 \times 2) + (30 \times \frac{1}{2}) = 60 + (30 \div 2)$

$60 + (30 \div 2) = 60 + 15$

$60 + 15 = 75$
                INCHES

➡ 75 INCHES

"Can I do the width?" Emma asked.

"Be my guest," Cam said, handing her the notebook.

"Since the width is just two belts, then it's a simple thirty times two. Sixty!" Emma shouted.

It may have been simple, but Gabe was still proud of his little sister and whispered, "Good job," to her.

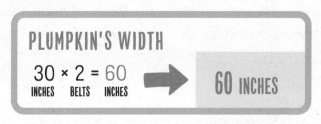

PLUMPKIN'S WIDTH

30 × 2 = 60
INCHES BELTS INCHES

➡ 60 INCHES

"Now you need the Over-the-Top Measurement, or the OTT," Abby said.

"Almost forgot," Cam said. "We just have to add up the three measurements, right?"

"Bingo," Abby said.

"I'd add sixty to seventy-five first," Cam said. "That's one hundred thirty-five. Then I add another hundred to that to get two hundred thirty-five inches as the OTT.

PLUMPKIN'S OTT

60 + 75 + 100 = 235
INCHES

➡ 235 INCHES

"Should we put the numbers into your app?" Emma asked, waving the notebook at her.

"Not yet," Abby said. "I think we should get the OTTs for all the pumpkins and then see if all the predicted weights line up."

"Is that the better way to do it mathematically?" Cam asked.

Abby shrugged. "No. But it's better dramatically."

Fair enough. They all liked drama. And so they started to do the calculations for the other OTTs.

"Wanna know how I would get the OTT?" Gabe asked Cam.

"There's a different way than what I did?" Cam said.

"An easier way, actually," Gabe said. "Abby already mentioned the distributive property. Instead of converting each measurement from belts to inches and then adding up the results, we can add up the lengths of all the belts first, and then do the conversion once we have the sum. It will result in the same number."

Cam put his hands on his hips and said, "Okay, genius. Show us."

"Happily," Gabe said, taking the notebook from his sister. "Orange Julius has a circumference of three belts, a height of one and two thirds belts, and a width of three and a half belts. So, I'm going to add up all the bolt lengths."

"But how do you add up one and two thirds and three and one half?" Cam asked. "Those are different fractions. Do you just add the top numbers and bottom numbers?"

"Nope," Gabe said. "That's what you do for multiplying and dividing fractions. For addition and subtraction, you need a common denominator."

"Denominator?" Cam said. "Is that a Marvel villain? Or DC?"

Gabe sighed and said, "Neither. It's the number on the bottom of the fraction. The top number is called the numerator, and the bottom number is called the denominator. The denominators have to match if you want to add or subtract fractions. And to make them match, you need to multiply them until they're the same number. That's known as a common denominator."

"What do you mean?" Cam said.

"In the case of the fractions two thirds and one half, we need to find a whole number that is divisible by the denominators, which are three and two."

"Divisibility!" Cam said. "Mrs. E. covered that yesterday. Six is divisible by three and two because three times two equals six!"

"And vice versa," Gabe said. "Two times three is also six. That's called the commutative property."

$$3 \times 2 = 6$$
$$2 \times 3 = 6$$

"So, what we need to do is multiply the denominator two by three and multiply the denominator three by two, and then both of the denominators will be six," Gabe went on.

"Don't forget the other step," Abby reminded him.

"I know, I know, I'm getting there," Gabe said. "Since we don't want the values of the fractions to change, we need to multiply the numerators, or the top numbers, by the same numbers."

"So, we multiply two thirds by two . . . halves?" Cam asked.

"Right," Gabe said. "And we multiply one half by three thirds. You'll notice that two over two and three over three are both equal to one, because any number divided by itself equals one."

Gabe wrote down an example.

$$\frac{2}{2} = 1$$
$$\frac{3}{3} = 1$$

"It's a clever way of multiplying the fractions by one, so they keep the same value, but the denominators change so we can use them in addition and subtraction," Gabe went on. "And once we do that, the equation is easy."

$$\frac{2}{3} \times \frac{2}{2} = \frac{4}{6}$$
$$\frac{1}{2} \times \frac{3}{3} = \frac{3}{6}$$
$$\frac{4}{6} + \frac{3}{6} = \frac{7}{6}$$

"Seven sixths are the same as one and one sixth, right?" Cam said. "Because there are six sixths in one and then you have one sixth left over."

$$\frac{7}{6} = \frac{6}{6} + \frac{1}{6}$$
$$\text{or}$$
$$1 + \frac{1}{6} = 1\frac{1}{6}$$

"You got it," Gabe said. "But let's not forget the original equation we were working on, figuring out Orange Julius's OTT. I'll write it out so it's easier to understand."

ORANGE JULIUS'S OTT

$$3 + 1\frac{2}{3} + 3\frac{1}{2}$$
BELTS   BELTS   BELTS

Cam grabbed the notebook and said, "I can do this. First, we add up the whole numbers."

$$3 + 1 + 3 = 7$$

"Then we add up the fractions," he went on.

$$2/3 + 1/2 = 4/6 + 3/6$$
$$4/6 + 3/6 = 7/6$$
$$7/6 = 1\,1/6$$

"And then we add them all together."

$$7 + 1\,1/6 = 8\,1/6$$
BELTS

"We still have to convert the belts to inches," Gabe said.

"I can handle that, too," Cam said. "Just multiply the belts by thirty. Start with thirty times eight. Then add thirty times one sixth, which is also thirty divided by six. And you get two hundred forty plus five. Or two hundred forty-five!"

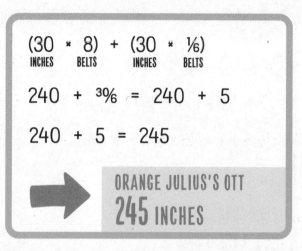

(30 × 8) + (30 × ⅙)
INCHES BELTS INCHES BELTS

$240 + {}^{30}\!/\!_6 = 240 + 5$

$240 + 5 = 245$

ORANGE JULIUS'S OTT
245 INCHES

"Well done," Abby said. "The only one left is Mr. Jiggles."

"Let me see if I can do this one," Emma said, grabbing the notebook from Cam. She methodically worked through the equation, using what she had just learned from her brother and his friends.

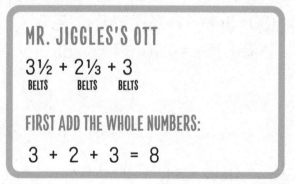

MR. JIGGLES'S OTT

3½ + 2⅓ + 3
BELTS BELTS BELTS

FIRST ADD THE WHOLE NUMBERS:

$3 + 2 + 3 = 8$

THEN ADD THE FRACTIONS BY FINDING
THE COMMON DENOMINATORS:

$$\tfrac{1}{2} + \tfrac{1}{3} = (\tfrac{1}{2} \times \tfrac{3}{3}) + (\tfrac{1}{3} \times \tfrac{2}{2})$$

$$(\tfrac{1}{2} \times \tfrac{3}{3}) + (\tfrac{1}{3} \times \tfrac{2}{2}) = \tfrac{3}{6} + \tfrac{2}{6}$$

$$\tfrac{3}{6} + \tfrac{2}{6} = \tfrac{5}{6}$$

THEN ADD THE WHOLE NUMBER
TO THE FRACTION:

$$8 + \tfrac{5}{6} = 8\tfrac{5}{6}$$
BELTS

THEN MULTIPLY THE BELTS BY 30 INCHES:

$$30 \times 8\tfrac{5}{6}$$
INCHES   BELTS

$$(30 \times 8) + (\tfrac{30}{1} \times \tfrac{5}{6}) = 240 + \tfrac{150}{6}$$
$$240 + \tfrac{150}{6} = 240 + 25 = 265$$

   MR. JIGGLES'S OTT
265 INCHES

"Wow," Gabe said. "I didn't know you had it in you!"

"I didn't, either, but I guess I do," Emma said with pride.

"I'm impressed with how you multiplied thirty by five sixths," Cam said. "How'd you know how to do that?"

"I guess I was listening to my brother for once," Emma said. "He said when you multiply fractions, you multiply the numerators by the numerators and the denominators by the denominators. And he said if you want to turn thirty into a fraction, all you had to do was make it thirty over one. Because thirty divided by one is thirty."

"Watch out, Gabe," Cam said. "Your sister might be taking your statistician jobs soon."

Gabe grumbled and said, "Let's not get ahead of ourselves. Besides, there are more pressing matters. We have to enter all the OTTs into Abby's app to see how accurate the weight predictions are."

Gabe showed Abby the numbers they'd written down and she pulled out an old phone. The phone didn't have Wi-Fi or even a working camera. But it had her app installed on it. The app was called WOW THAT'S A BIG PUMPKIN!

She plugged the numbers one by one into

the WOW THAT'S A BIG PUMPKIN app. She announced the results as she went.

"We already calculated General Humongulo's stats, but let's review them again," Abby said. "The recorded weight was four hundred thirteen pounds. The app told us that the estimated weight was four hundred eight pounds. So, the difference between the estimated weight and the real weight was five pounds."

"Pretty good," Gabe said as he wrote it down.

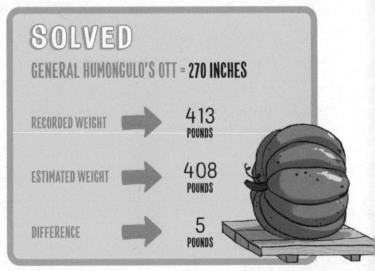

SOLVED

GENERAL HUMONGULO'S OTT = **270 INCHES**

RECORDED WEIGHT ➡ 413 POUNDS

ESTIMATED WEIGHT ➡ 408 POUNDS

DIFFERENCE ➡ 5 POUNDS

"Onto Plumpkin," Abby said. "The recorded weight was two hundred eighty-two pounds. The estimated weight, according to my app, is two hundred seventy-eight pounds. So that's a difference of four pounds."

"Even better," Cam said.

PLUMPKIN'S OTT = 235 INCHES

RECORDED WEIGHT ➡ 282 POUNDS

ESTIMATED WEIGHT ➡ 278 POUNDS

DIFFERENCE ➡ 4 POUNDS

"For Orange Julius, we have a recorded weight of three hundred six pounds and an estimated weight of three hundred twelve pounds. The difference? Six pounds." Abby said.

"Still pretty close," Emma said.

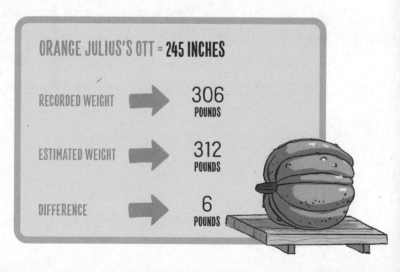

ORANGE JULIUS'S OTT = 245 INCHES

RECORDED WEIGHT ➡ 306 POUNDS

ESTIMATED WEIGHT ➡ 312 POUNDS

DIFFERENCE ➡ 6 POUNDS

"Finally, Mr. Jiggles," Abby said. "Recorded: four hundred thirty pounds. Estimated: three hundred eighty-seven. Difference: forty-three pounds."

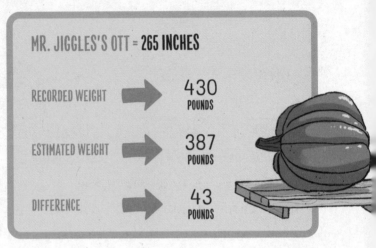

MR. JIGGLES'S OTT = **265 INCHES**

RECORDED WEIGHT ➡ 430 POUNDS

ESTIMATED WEIGHT ➡ 387 POUNDS

DIFFERENCE ➡ 43 POUNDS

"Whoa," Gabe and Emma said at the same time.

"Sounds like I'm not the only one who's suspicious of Mr. Jiggles," Abby said.

A knowing smile bloomed on Cam's face. "And I know why he's called Mr. Jiggles. Come on."

Then Cam took off running again.

Chapter 11

THE CASE OF THE EXTRA PUMPKIN POUNDS

Again, it was hard to keep up with Cam. His training for *Triumph or Caketastrophe* was making him almost too nimble. Not a bad thing, usually, but Abby, Gabe, and Emma nearly lost him as they wove through the festival crowd, finally ending at . . . A trash can?

By the time they reached it, Cam had already tipped over the trash can where Abby had found her Jell-O box earlier. He was sifting through the trash, stacking up the empty Jell-O boxes, and counting out loud.

" . . . twenty-two, twenty-three, twenty-four . . ."

"What's he doing?" Emma whispered to Gabe, and Gabe shrugged.

But Abby's face lit up. "I think I know. Let him finish."

So, they stayed quiet until he had counted them all.

"Thirty-one," Cam said.

"Thirty-two, actually," Abby said as she pulled the empty box of Jell-O from her pocket. Before tossing it onto the pile, she looked at the instructions and smiled.

"What are you smiling for?" Gabe said, picking up a box and examining it. "So, we have thirty-two boxes of Jell-O? What does that have to do with . . . Ohhh!"

Suddenly, Gabe understood, too.

"What am I not getting?" Emma said.

"You'll see," Cam said. "Gabe and Abby, can you collect all the other clues we've found today? I think it's time we saved the fall festival."

"I was going to say the same thing," Gabe said.

"Let's go," Abby said.

And the two of them were off without another word, leaving a confused Emma still standing next to Cam.

"What can I do?" Emma asked.

"Can you be loud and persuasive?" Cam said.

"Those are my two best qualities," Emma said.

"Good," Cam said. "I want you to spread the word throughout the fair to have everyone meet us at the pumpkin patch."

"I'm on it," Emma said. Then she was off, too.

Cam cleaned up the trash he had dumped over, flattened out the empty boxes of Jell-O, and then carried them over to the pumpkin patch. By lining up and stacking some extra wooden pallets and plywood, he built a makeshift stage. Almost as soon as he was finished, Abby and Gabe arrived, depositing the following items on the stage:

▶ The empty can of black paint

▶ The funnel

▶ The receipt with the note on it

▶ The apple corer

▶ The registration sheet for Mr. Jiggles

▶ The frozen pie that Cam couldn't eat

The Prime Detectives then huddled together and discussed what they were each thinking. Before long, a large crowd had arrived. Emma had done her job, and with the help of Cam's sisters, she had gathered everyone at the fair around the pumpkin patch. It was time for the Prime Detectives to present their case. It was time for them to save the fall festival from a full fiasco.

"Hear ye, hear ye!" Cam called out as he used the metal apple corer to bang on the empty can of black paint like it was a bell. "We, the Prime Detectives, have some proclamations to make! Lend us your ears!"

Cam's display was amusing for Abby and embarrassing for Gabe. All that mattered, however, was that it worked. The crowd quieted and looked up at the three kids standing on the makeshift stage. Gabe cleared his throat and spoke.

"We regret to inform you, but the fall festival has been sabotaged," he said.

He expected people to gasp in shock and horror, but most people simply appeared confused. So, he elaborated.

"First, the tickets went missing," he said. "Then the dunk tank was compromised."

"The lemonade stand ran out of water," Abby said next. "And the pies for the pie-eating contest were frozen."

"Black paint ruined the voting for the pie-baking competition," Cam said. "And we haven't even gotten to Mr. Jiggles and that miscarriage of justice."

"Who's Mr. Jiggles?" Sanjeev called out from the crowd.

"He's this fella right here behind me," Abby said, pointing over her shoulder.

"He weighed the most out of any of the pumpkins," Gabe said. "But no one knows who entered him in the competition. Anyone out there wanna claim Mr. Jiggles?"

Heads turned. Chatter filled the crowd. But no one stepped forward to say they were the person who entered Mr. Jiggles in the contest.

"Well then," Cam said as he walked over to Mr. Jiggles with the apple corer in his hand. "I guess no one will mind if I do this."

Then Cam stabbed Mr. Jiggles.

That's right.

He plunged the apple corer deep into Mr. Jiggles's orange flesh!

Now people gasped. And they gasped even louder when Cam pulled the apple corer out. Because orange liquid poured from the hole he created.

"Mr. Jiggles is bleeding!" Mason screamed.

Cam shrugged and then stuck his finger into the stream of orange liquid. Licking his finger, he smiled and said, "Exactly as I suspected."

"And Cam is drinking Mr. Jiggles's blood!" Grayson yelled.

"Don't worry, it's only Jell-O," Abby said.

"Pumpkins have Jell-O for blood!" Jason screamed.

It was clear that this could soon get out of hand. So, Cam waved his arms and shouted, "The pumpkin is fine. Please listen and we'll explain what's happened."

The Prime Detectives were not perfect. They made mistakes. But when they were about to solve a mystery, people knew it was smart to listen. So, people listened.

"Someone filled Mr. Jiggles with Jell-O and that made the pumpkin heavier," Gabe told them. "It was a way of cheating and winning the pumpkin-growing contest."

"But Jell-O isn't liquid," Noah said. "It's jiggly."

"Only if you make it with a combination of boiling water and cold water," Cam said. "Whoever filled Mr. Jiggles with Jell-O didn't add boiling water. They used cold water from the lemonade stand. Therefore, Mr. Jiggles isn't very jiggly."

A hand shot up from the crowd. Abby scanned the scene and realized it was their teacher, Mrs. E. "Do you have a question, Mrs. E.?"

"Can you tell everyone how you knew there was Jell-O inside the pumpkin?" Mrs. E. said.

"Math," Abby said plainly. "There's a

formula to estimate the weight of the pumpkins using their circumferences, heights, and widths. And we knew the estimated weight of Mr. Jiggles should've been around four to six pounds within the actual weight. But the difference was forty-three pounds. Naturally, we were suspicious of those extra pounds."

"There were some empty boxes of Jell-O in a nearby trash can," Gabe said, waving a flat, empty box in the air. "And the lemonade stand was missing some of its water."

"We also found an apple corer and a funnel," Cam said. "So, I surmised that someone must've cut a hole in Mr. Jiggles with the apple corer, then used the funnel to fill it with the Jell-O and the water, and then plugged the hole back up with the core they created."

"Cam surmised correctly!" Abby said. "It was confirmed by the math."

"That's right," Cam said. "We counted the empty boxes of Jell-O, and we looked at the instructions. Each box contained three ounces of Jell-O mix in it," Cam said. "To turn each box into solid Jell-O, someone needed to add two cups of water. A cup of water is eight fluid ounces, which actually weighs a little more than eight solid ounces, but we didn't worry about that. To us, eight ounces was eight ounces. We didn't need to be exact."

"Close was good enough," Abby said.

"So, there were thirty-two boxes of Jell-O," Cam went on. "Three ounces of mix in each box. Two cups of water needed to be added to each three-ounce mix. If someone made all thirty-two boxes of Jell-O, how much would it weigh, Abby?"

"Thirty-eight pounds," Abby said immediately. "Which is just five pounds less than the forty-three pounds we were suspicious about. Well within the range of expected estimates."

The crowd stared at the Prime Detectives. Everyone was obviously trying to process all the information they'd just heard. Mrs. E. raised her hand again.

"Yes, Mrs. E.?" Abby said.

"I think we're going to need you to show your work," Mrs. E. said.

"We figured you'd say that," Gabe said. "So, we wrote it all out on the blackboard."

Gabe flipped around the blackboard that had been displaying the weights of the pumpkins. It was now filled with their equations.

CONVERSION CHART

JELL-O MIX

$$1 \text{ CUP OF WATER} = 8 \text{ FLUID OUNCES}$$

(approxiamtely 8 ounces of solid weight)

$$16 \text{ OUNCES} = 1 \text{ POUND}$$

$$2 + 3 = (2 \times 8) + 3$$

CUPS OF WATER   OUNCES OF JELL-O MIX   FLUID OUNCES   OUNCES

$$(2 \times 8) + 3 = 16 + 3$$

OUNCES   OUNCES

$$16 + 3 = 19$$

OUNCES OF MIXED JELL-O PER BOX

$$32 \times 19 = 608$$

BOXES OF JELL-O   OUNCES OF MIXED JELL-O PER BOX   TOTAL OUNCES

$$608 \div 16 = 38$$

OUNCES   OUNCES   POUNDS OF JELL-O

Mrs. E. clapped. "Well done, kids. Well done."

"But what does it tell us besides that someone cheated?" Kiko asked.

"This is more than cheating," Gabe said. "Based on the evidence we collected, including a handwriting analysis from my little sister, we have discovered that the same person is responsible for hiding the tickets, making Emmett and Luciana miss their shots at the dunk tank, stealing the water from the lemonade stand, freezing the pies, pouring paint on the colored plates, and filling Mr. Jiggles with Jell-O."

"But who would do such a thing?" Maisie asked.

"Funny you should ask," Cam said.

"Because we're pretty sure it was you," Abby said.

For a moment, Maisie stood there motionless. Then her body started to tremble. Finally, a storm of words erupted from inside her.

"They're right! They're always right! I did it! I did it all! I ruined the fall festival!"

When the surprised murmur of the crowd quieted down, Maisie trudged up to the stage.

She was slow but deliberate. Like this was something she knew was coming eventually. And now she had no choice but to confront it. With her head hung low, she began to speak.

"I'm not proud of what I did," Maisie said.

"Can you tell us exactly what you did?" Abby asked.

Maisie nodded and said, "A lot of things. First, I'm the person who grew Mr. Jiggles. Which took all summer and fall."

"Even if it's not the real winner, it's still an impressive gourd," Cam said.

Abby nodded in agreement.

"A family friend with a pickup truck brought Mr. Jiggles and me to the fair really early," Maisie said. "It was before anyone else was here. As soon as the friend left, I cut a hole in Mr. Jiggles with the apple corer, put the funnel in the hole, and filled it with Jell-O mix and water from the lemonade stand. I spilled a bunch of water, but I got enough in."

"Spilled water explains some of the mud we found on the ground near the pumpkins," Gabe said.

"And cold water explains why the Jell-O never solidified," Cam said.

"I thought it would harden up and then if

someone poked a hole in the pumpkin, they wouldn't know that it was filled with something," Maisie said with a sigh. "Or if they shook it, they wouldn't hear water sloshing around."

"You needed half of the water to be boiling," Cam said.

"Even if I did know that, I didn't have time to boil water," Maisie said. "Because as soon as I filled Mr. Jiggles with the Jell-O and the cold water, all the other pumpkins showed up. So, I plugged the hole up with the piece of pumpkin from the apple corer, and then I taped the paperwork over the spot so no one would notice."

"Smart thinking," Abby said. "Even though it was cheating."

"What'd you do next?" Gabe asked.

"Well, a baker had just delivered the cherry pies," Maisie said. "So, when no one was looking, I swapped the fresh ones with frozen ones I bought at the store."

"And you left the funnel and the apple corer behind on the pie cart, right?" Cam said as he held up the two objects.

"I guess so," Maisie said. "I was in a rush. Because I had more to do. Next, I took a can of black paint and poured it into the bin where people would vote for their favorite apple pies. I knew it would make counting the votes impossible. Then I went to the ticket booth and grabbed the tickets, because I was going to throw them out. I was carrying them away from the fair when my sister showed up. I didn't want her to know what I was doing, so I stashed the tickets and the can of paint in a bush near the parking lot. That's where she eventually found the tickets."

"And where I found the can of paint," Abby said, holding it up.

"I rushed back to the ticket booth," Maisie said. "And people started to arrive. I had to give them the bad news that there were no tickets to sell."

"That must've been when I arrived," a voice called out from the crowd.

All eyes turned to a boy at the back. It was Emmett.

"He's right," Maisie said. "Emmett was one of the first people here. I had asked him to do me a favor yesterday, but I didn't have a chance to thank him."

"And that favor was missing all his shots at the dunk tank, right?" Gabe said.

"Exactly," Emmett admitted. "Maisie said

she had overhead on the playground that people were gonna give me and Luciana their tickets for the dunk tank. She assured me that missing our shots was the best way to sell more tickets for the fair and get more money for Ricky's Rhinos. If I kept missing, people would keep buying tickets. I convinced Luciana of the same thing."

"He's right," Maisie said. "I did tell him that. Even though it wasn't true. It was always my plan to refund people for the missed shots. I felt bad for tricking you, Emmett. But I had to. And I had to thank you, so that's why I passed you a note. I couldn't thank you out loud and make everyone suspicious."

Gabe held up the receipt. "And here's the note. It says, *Thanks for the bad aim. You're an Awesomesaurus!* It's on the back of a receipt with a black fingerprint on it."

"That was the only paper I had," Maisie said. "I had bought the Jell-O and frozen pies the day before, and the receipt was still in the pocket of my jacket."

Cam peered over at the receipt in Gabe's hand, and suddenly it made sense. The letters on the receipt were obviously abbreviations, and Cam translated them in his head.

32 QTY OGDM—$48.00

(32 Quantity of Orange Gelatin Dessert Mix—$48.00)

10 QTY FRZ CP—$80.00

(10 Quantity of Frozen Cherry Pies—$80.00)

"I think we probably showed up shortly after that," Abby said.

"You're probably right," Maisie said. "And I should've known you would catch me. You always figure things out. But how did you know it was me?"

The Prime Detectives all looked at each other. Cam, never one to be shy, took the lead.

"It was simple, really," he said. "First we linked all the clues together because the black fingerprint on the receipt matched the black paint in the can, which was found next to the tickets."

"And the handwriting on the note and the handwriting on paperwork for Mr. Jiggles matched," Gabe said. "Thank you to my little sister for figuring that out."

Emma smiled and proudly said, "I also figured out that the culprit was left-handed."

"A great clue that narrowed our suspect list down by a lot," Abby said. "Only ten percent of the population is left-handed."

"We know that Emmett is left-handed because that's how he shoots the basketball," Cam said. "But we didn't think he'd write a note thanking himself."

"Basic odds tell us that since there are fewer than twenty kids in our class, only one or two other people in our class are probably left-handed," Gabe said.

"And we all noticed yesterday when you were giving money back to Kiko, you used your left hand," Abby said.

"Obviously, it could've been someone who wasn't in our class who sabotaged the fair," Cam said. "But in the note, you called Emmett an awesomesaurus. That's a term Emmett made up in class yesterday. It was his name for an imaginary thirteenth month of the year. Only someone in our class would remember that."

"Finally, we knew you had better access to the fair than almost anyone," Abby said. "Because it's supporting your uncle Ricky's conservation project. The one that's saving the black rhinoceroses of Eswatini."

"There's just one thing we couldn't figure out, though," Gabe said.

"Why'd you do it?" all three of the Prime Detectives said at the same time.

Maisie paused for a moment. She took a deep breath. Then she said something that no one expected.

"Because there are no such things as black rhinoceroses. And there's no country named Eswatini. Ricky's Rhinos is fake."

No one knew how to respond to that. Well, no one except for one person.

Maisie's uncle Ricky was standing at the back of the crowd. And he was laughing.

Chapter 12

RICKY'S RHINOS

Ricky was a tall man with a bright smile and a thick beard. The Prime Detectives had met him before. He was a wildlife expert, and a friend to Mrs. E. and the custodian, Mrs. Vernon. He had helped the school once, but that was a story for another day.

Today, at the fall festival, Ricky wasn't helping. He was laughing. At his niece Maisie, no less. And Maisie was not happy about it.

"Why are you laughing at me, Uncle Ricky?" she said. "Can't you just admit it's true? Ricky's Rhinos doesn't exist."

When he finally gathered himself, Ricky responded. "And why would you think it doesn't exist?"

"Because of two things. The first thing happened a few days ago," Maisie said, and she turned to the crowd to explain. "My uncle works for the wildlife sanctuary in town. They have a few animals from other countries, but mostly they help local animals like foxes and raccoons and turtles."

"It's a lovely place," Mrs. Vernon told everyone.

"It is," Maisie said. "They even have some garden plots there that they let the public use. That's where I grew Mr. Jiggles. I did a good job growing him, too, even though I was pretty sure I didn't have a chance to beat Abby. I need you to know that I never planned to cheat in the pumpkin-growing contest. At least not until I discovered something disturbing."

"Disturbing?" Cam said with a gulp. "What was disturbing?"

"This," Maisie said, picking up the can of black paint. "I found this in a toolshed at the wildlife sanctuary. It has the word DICEROS on it."

She showed it to everyone, and the word was clearly written on it.

"What does *diceros* mean?" Abby asked.

"It's a scientific name for *rhinoceros*," Maisie said. "Remember how my uncle Ricky promised everyone that there would be a black rhinoceros at the wildlife sanctuary? And that the winners of the contests at the fall festival would get to meet that rhinoceros? Well, let me ask you this.

Has anyone ever seen even a picture of a rhinoceros that is black?"

People in the crowd seemed to be considering this question, but Mrs. E. was the only one to answer. "Maisie is technically right. All rhinoceroses are a shade of either gray or brown."

"Unless you paint them," Maisie said. "There *is* a rhino at the sanctuary, but she's light gray. Her name is Honey, and she's the most exotic animal they have there. Honey is a *big* deal. So, when I found that can of black paint, I began to suspect that my uncle Ricky was going to paint Honey. To make her look like a 'black' rhino."

Abby's eyes went wide. "That's a big accusation."

"I know," Maisie said. "But as I told you before, there were two things. And the other thing is something I discovered yesterday. When Mrs. E. was giving us her lesson on the thirteen-month calendar, she set a globe down on my desk. I looked at the globe and the continent of Africa. I looked as closely as anyone possibly could. And I can assure you of one thing. There was no country on the globe called Eswatini. It simply doesn't exist. Ricky made it up."

"So, what exactly are you saying?" Gabe asked.

Ricky had been listening quietly to his niece make her accusations, and she turned to him with a sympathetic face and said, "I'm saying that Ricky is a good person. But he's chosen a tough job. My parents have told me that the wildlife sanctuary often struggles to bring in money. So, I think Ricky made up a fake charity about a fake animal from a fake country. Because it sounded better than asking for more money to help the ordinary animals that most people can usually see in their backyards."

Ricky sniffled and cleared his throat. Obviously, he was upset. "So, you think I was trying to steal money?"

Maisie shook her head. "No. No. I thought you made a bad decision. I decided that rather than expose you and get you in trouble, I'd make sure everyone either didn't buy tickets, or they got their money back. I made sure all the contests were ruined so that no one would go to the sanctuary and you wouldn't have to trick them by painting Honey. I sabotaged the festival for everyone's sake. And for yours."

Ricky sniffled again. Then he walked up onto the makeshift stage. He put an arm around Maisie, and he kissed her on the forehead. "You're a sweet kid," he said.

"I'm sorry I had to tell everyone," Maisie said. "I tried to keep it a secret."

"That's all right," Ricky said. "There's no secret to keep. The sanctuary is doing fine. In fact, since Honey arrived, we've had more donations than ever. I started Ricky's Rhinos because of Honey. She inspired it. She *is* a black rhinoceros, after all."

"No," Maisie said. "She's clearly light gray."

"The name *black rhinoceros* is a reference to the dark mud they roll in to cool themselves down," Ricky said. "It doesn't have anything to do with their actual color. It's also a way to distinguish them from white rhinoceroses, which are also gray."

Maisie's eyebrows went up. "Okay, that's confusing. Then what was the black paint for?"

"For the wall around Honey's enclosure," Ricky said. "It needed a fresh coat. We put the word *diceros* on it because that's how her area at the sanctuary is labeled on our maps."

"That still doesn't explain the country of Eswatini," Gabe said. "I'll be honest with you. I'd never heard of that country until the fall festival. And I'm pretty good at geography."

"I bet you are," Ricky said. "And so is Maisie. I know what she saw is true. I'm quite certain that Mrs. E.'s globe doesn't have the country of Eswatini on it, either."

"Why?" Cam said. "Because you made it up?"

"No," Ricky said with a laugh. "Because up until a few years ago, Eswatini had a different name."

"I bought my globe when I first became a teacher," Mrs. E. said. "That was over ten years ago."

"Ten years ago, Eswatini was known as Swaziland," Ricky said. "But recently, on the fiftieth anniversary of the country's independence, the king changed their name to something more traditional to their language. The country became Eswatini, which means *place of the Swazi people*."

"Oh," Maisie said. "I didn't know that."

"I wouldn't expect you to," Ricky said, and he gave his niece another hug.

"So, this was all a misunderstanding?" Cam asked.

"Which probably could've been solved with a Google search," Gabe said.

Abby wagged a finger. "Maybe, but I think there's more to it than that. To become a good detective, you definitely have to use your instincts like Maisie did, but more importantly you have to *rely* on the evidence. Maisie thought she had evidence, but what did she have, really? An idea about rhinoceroses and an old globe. Certainly not enough to accuse her uncle and ruin the day for everyone."

"We're all still learning to be good detectives," Cam added. "And one thing that always helps me to become a better one is talking to people. You didn't talk to anyone, Maisie. You should've shared your concerns with someone else before doing anything."

Maisie nodded and hung her head, because these were good points, and she was embarrassed.

"You can always talk to me," Ricky told Maisie. "I'll always give you the full story."

"I know that now," Maisie said. "And I will."

"So, what are we going to do about the fall festival and all the contests?" Gabe asked.

"Maisie said she switched the pies," Cam said. "Where did you put the fresh ones? If we pulled them out, maybe we could still have the pie-eating contest."

"Not so sure about that," Abby said, motioning with her chin to the crowd. "I think the fresh pies have already been found."

The offensive line of the football team (otherwise known as Desmond, Sal, Manny, Conner, and Blake) sat in the grass. Each guy had two empty pie plates on the ground in front of him and cherry-colored stains around his mouth.

"Sorry," Desmond said.

"We were hungry," Sal said.

"But we can confirm that they were delicious," Manny said.

Conner and Blake didn't say anything because their mouths were still full, but they nodded in agreement.

"I wish someone had timed them," Gabe said.

"All I know is that I didn't stand a chance," Cam said.

Abby put a hand on both their shoulders and said, "Don't worry. I'm sure there will be plenty of pumpkin pie to practice on soon."

Six days later, a bus pulled up in front of Arithmos Elementary. A line of fourth graders stood waiting for it. Sanjeev and Emmett were the first two in line. And they were both dressed in orange. It was the second Friday of the month, after all.

The bus was taking the kids on a field trip. They were all going to the wildlife sanctuary where Maisie's uncle Ricky worked. They were all going to meet Honey the black rhinoceros.

And not only that, but they were all going to get another shot at dunking Mrs. E. The dunk tank had been moved to the garden plot where Maisie had grown Mr. Jiggles. Sadly, they couldn't do the entire fall festival all over again, but this was almost as good.

Wearing her UNSINKABLE MRS. E.! swim dress, Mrs. E. ushered the kids aboard. The Prime Detectives stood in the middle of the line, next to Maisie. They had forgiven Maisie, of course. And Ricky's Rhinos had ended up raising even more money than expected. Everyone at the festival had pitched in some extra cash. They didn't care that the festival was a fiasco. They simply wanted to help a good cause.

"The pumpkin pies were tasty," Cam said. "But I still think we should've taken Mr. Jiggles and General Humongulo and done some punkin' chunkin' with them."

"I think we should've cut them into boats and had a pumpkin regatta," Gabe said. "Much easier than building a giant catapult. I mean, do you even know how to build a catapult?"

Cam shrugged. "How hard could it be?"

Abby knew exactly how hard it could be, and she was about to provide some information on levers and fulcrums and so on, but suddenly there was a tap on her shoulder. She turned around to see Principal Barnes.

"Oh, hi, Principal Barnes," Abby said.

"Can I speak to you for a minute?" Principal Barnes said. "Don't worry. You won't miss the field trip."

"Sure," Abby said, because while Principal Barnes was sometimes intimidating, there was no reason to believe he was there to deliver bad news.

So, Abby and Principal Barnes stepped to the side for a moment to have a discussion. The others were too far away to hear what they were saying.

"Do you think this is about that special test Abby took last week?" Cam asked Gabe.

"I'd entirely forgotten about that," Gabe said. "I bet it is."

Abby's back was to them, so they couldn't read any clues from her face to tell if she was happy or sad. But the conversation didn't last very long, and when she turned around, the look on her face was obvious. She was surprised.

"So . . . ?" Gabe and Cam asked at the same time.

It took Abby a few moments to collect herself. When she finally did, she said, "I can't tell you much. All I can tell you is that things are going to get . . . weird."

"Weird good?" Cam asked.

"Or weird bad?" Gabe asked.

"Just weird weird," Abby said.

She left it at that.

It was time for them to get on the bus. It was time to enjoy a visit to the wildlife sanctuary. It was time for them to have a little fun before things got weird.

In other words, it was just another autumn day for the Prime Detectives.

MORE MYSTERIES TO UNRAVEL!

Join the Prime Detectives in

Math Mysteries

THE TRIPLET THREAT

Available wherever books are sold.